BURNED BY DARKNESS

BOOK ONE
DRAGONS OF
ETERNITY

ALEXANDRA IVY

Burned by Darkness
© 2015 by by Debbie Raleigh

Editor: Julia Ganis
– JuliaEdits.com

Cover art and formatting by
Sweet 'N Spicy Designs
– http://sweetnspicydesigns.com

http://alexandraivy.com

To all my devoted readers who have inspired the Guardians over the years. I hope you love my dragons just as much!

CHAPTER ONE

"Are the shades lowered?"

Tayla's lips twitched at the sound of the French-accented voice that floated from the attics.

"I'm doing it now," she called back, pressing the button near the door that would slide thin panels over the windows that blocked out direct sunlight while still allowing her a clear view.

It was a bonus feature that she'd had installed only last week. She might be an imp who adored the warm rays shining into every room, but her current houseguest turned to stone in the sun.

She hadn't been looking for a companion. Heck, she hadn't been looking for a house.

After all, she'd spent the past twenty-five years on the run, constantly aware that she was being hunted.

That overwhelming sense of being stalked had been like a dark cloud hovering over her head, forcing her from one hiding place to another.

But from the second she'd caught sight of the large Victorian home just south of Chicago she hadn't been able to get it out of her head.

The three-story house had the usual wings and bays, with a wraparound porch, gabled roof and gingerbread wood trim. It was painted a pretty pink with white shutters, and was surrounded by a large garden and rolling vineyards that gave a sense of peaceful isolation.

It was charming.

And serene.

And everything she'd ever wanted in a home.

Plus it had the added benefit of being a perfect spot to set up an elegant teahouse.

Giving in to the rare impulse, Tayla purchased the property and hired a witch to come and wrap several disguise spells around the property. As an imp, she had her own fey magic—specifically, enchanting items so her customers would crave her delicate pastries—but she couldn't create complicated spells.

She needed to make sure she was well hidden from her stalker—or perhaps it was *stalkers*—if she intended to stay in one place more than a few days.

Over the past months she hadn't regretted her choice to settle down, although she'd discovered that she didn't enjoy being alone in the large house at night.

She wasn't afraid. Not exactly.

She was more…restless.

Which no doubt explained why she'd given in to the persuasion of the miniature gargoyle who'd unexpectedly arrived on her doorstep two weeks ago.

She smiled as the door that led to the attic was pushed open and a tiny creature who stood no more than three feet tall waddled into the room.

He had the usual gray, leathery skin and grotesque gargoyle features, complete with horns and a long tail he kept meticulously polished. His wings, however, were anything but usual.

Larger than normal, they were as lacy as the wings of a dew fairy and swirled with brilliant blues and crimsons and gold.

He also had a charming French accent and a habit of making her laugh when he mangled the English language.

He'd requested rooms in the attic for his brand-spanking-new dating service, and she'd agreed. Why not? It would bring in additional customers, and she wouldn't be alone every night.

It was an arrangement that'd worked out well.

Now he followed her as she moved through the front salon filled with overstuffed chairs and round tables covered by frilly doilies. With a brisk efficiency, she made sure the cups and dishes had all been returned to the china cabinets and that the floral carpets were vacuumed.

Then, together they headed down the short hall and entered the kitchen she'd had remodeled after moving in. The large room had a white tiled floor and open-beam ceiling where copper pans were hanging from long hooks. The appliances were all top of the line, stainless steel that'd cost her a fortune. And in the middle of the floor were long, wooden tables that she'd hand-carved with fey glyphs to add the enchantments to her pastries.

Best of all, the far wall had a bank of windows that overlooked the heavily wooded acreage that'd come with the property.

She paused to admire the sight of the trees in full autumn glory. Her fey blood ached to be surrounded by nature even as she appreciated all the modern conveniences.

There was a soft ding as her oven timer warned her she needed to remove the scones she'd prepared for their late tea. Since Levet's arrival she'd encouraged him to share at least one meal a day with her. It was a genuine pleasure not to have to eat alone.

Grabbing a towel, she reached in to pull out a tray, setting it on the table just as the demon held up his hand to reveal the bottle he'd had hidden behind his back.

"Ta'da." He gave a wave of the bottle.

Tayla tossed aside the towel, studying her companion with a faint smile.

"What's that?"

"My favorite wine."

Tayla wrinkled her nose, watching Levet move to take a seat at the table near the windows.

"I'm not much of a drinker," she told him.

"You will like this, I promise," he assured her. "Besides, we are celebrating."

Hmm. That was news to her.

"What are we celebrating?"

"I had my first satisfied customer."

"Ah." With a small smile, Tayla placed the scones on a plate and gathered two wine glasses. "That is of course a reason to celebrate. Tell me about your satisfied client."

Levet's wings twitched with pride. "I managed to find a perfect match for a beautiful young ice sprite who'd been living alone in the Arctic," he informed her. "I connected her with a fire sprite who has been eager to start a family." He heaved a deep sigh. "It was love at first sight."

Fire and ice?

Tayla gave an inward shrug. Perhaps opposites truly did attract.

Moving to the table, she set down the plate of scones and allowed Levet to pour them both a glass of the amber wine. With an unabashed eagerness, the gargoyle reached for one of the delicate pastries.

"*Ma belle*, these are *très bien*," he sighed, eating the scone in one large bite. He demolished two more before he lifted his glass. "A toast to success."

"To success," she murmured, taking a cautious sip of the wine. She lifted her brows as she tasted the hint of nectar that was blended into the expensive vintage. The bottle had to have cost the gargoyle a small fortune. "Yum," she breathed, taking a deeper sip. "Where did you get this?"

Over the years she'd bought small vials of nectar, but since she was desperately trying to save every penny she could get her hands on to keep a roof over her head, it was a rare occurrence.

Now she savored the warmth that spread through her.

The gray eyes returned to study her with an unexpected intensity, starting at the top of her dark gold hair that spilled over her shoulders and down her back with hints of fire in the silken strands. From there he moved to the pale oval of her face, lingering on the light green eyes with fissures of jade before taking in the narrow nose and the plush peach lips.

He took a minute to approve of her slender body, casually attired in a pair of ivory slacks with a cashmere sweater that she'd matched with a pearl necklace, before he answered.

"I have a direct connection to the King of the Fey."

Tayla made a choked sound. She'd heard rumors that the rare pureblooded fey had returned to this dimension, but she hadn't been fortunate enough to catch a glimpse of one.

"How could you be acquainted with the Chantri?" she demanded.

Levet took a sip of his wine. "Not that I like to toot my own horny, but—"

"Horn," Tayla corrected with a twitch of her lips. "Toot your own horn."

"Horn or horny, it is all the same thing." Levet blithely waved a clawed hand. "The point is that I have saved the world on more than one occasion and I have several VIDs who are deeply in my debt."

Tayla blinked in confusion. "VIDs?"

"Very Important Demons." Levet gave a preening flap of his wings. "Including the King of Vampires and the King of Weres."

Tayla furrowed her brow. She hated to doubt the tiny demon's honesty, but it seemed a stretch to believe that he was actually acquainted with such important creatures.

"If you have such powerful friends then why did you choose to set up your dating service in this isolated neighborhood?" she asked, truly curious. "Wouldn't it have made more sense to be somewhere you could use your connections to attract customers?"

The gargoyle wrinkled his small snout. "There might have been the teeniest, tiniest misunderstanding when I opened my business in Viper's club."

"Viper." Tayla tilted her head to the side. She'd heard that name before. "The vampire clan chief of Chicago?"

"*Oui*. He is a selfish pain in the *derrière*."

"What happened?"

Levet hunched his shoulder. "I was considerate enough to chose his club, the Viper Pit, as the location for my dating service. I even threw a party to celebrate my new business. But did he thank me? *Non*. He claimed the bottles of champagne I'd borrowed from his cellar were some priceless vintage and tossed me out the door. Fah. He even threatened to have my head mounted on his wall if he caught sight of me." Levet took a deep drink of his wine. "It seemed best to avoid Chicago for a few weeks." He cleared his throat. "Or centuries."

Tayla's lips twitched. Although she found the tiny creature amusing, she knew there were other demons who weren't quite so tolerant of his eccentric personality. Including the nearby wood sprite who'd threatened to neuter him if he caught Levet near his daughter again.

"And that's when you decided to come here?"

"It is a lovely location," he said, glancing toward the view of the lush countryside. "Of course I did not fully consider that it would be too remote to encourage drop-dead customers."

Tayla blinked. Drop-dead? Zombies? Did they actually date? Oh…wait.

"Drop-in customers."

"*Oui*, drop-in." Setting aside his glass, Levet studied her with a sudden hint of curiosity. "It makes me wonder why you would choose such an isolated spot to open your teahouse."

"I'm hardly isolated," she pointed out, taking another drink. The wine was loosening the tension that had been a part of her life for as long as she could remember. "I have hundreds of customers who visit the shop."

Levet clicked his tongue in disapproval. "Customers are not the same as family or friends."

She shrugged. She'd never actually had a friend. Heck, she hadn't had a real home until she'd bought this house. And even now her bags remained packed and located next to her bedroom door.

Being ready for a quick exit seemed like a good idea.

"They are to me."

Levet blinked at her blunt honesty, then something that was perilously close to pity rippled over his ugly little face.

"And what about love?"

She stiffened. "Excuse me?"

Levet tilted his head to the side, rubbing one of his nubby horns.

"I can accept that you have made friends with several of your customers. Many of them are quite charming," he said. "And I, better than anyone, comprehend a desire to avoid your family. They can be…"

"Difficult?" Tayla offered when his words trailed away.

"Homicidal."

Ummm. Okay. Tayla regarded her companion with a newfound curiosity.

She'd thought her childhood had been shitty. At least her family hadn't actually tried to kill her.

Was that what had drawn her to the little demon?

Had she sensed they were both wounded by their pasts?

"Yeah, families suck," she muttered.

Levet reached across the table to brush a claw lightly over the back of her clenched hand.

"But such a young and beautiful woman should have a true mate who worships you."

With a panicked surge, Tayla was on her feet. "No," she breathed in horror.

Levet blinked in surprise. "*Non?*"

Tayla's stomach cramped with fear. "The last thing I want is a mate."

A long silence filled the room before her companion asked the obvious question.

"Why would you say such a thing?"

"Because it's the truth." She shivered, recalling a pair of amber eyes that had smoldered with cruel arrogance even as his touch had promised paradise. "Why would I want some arrogant, pig-headed, ill-mannered male thinking he owns me?"

The gray eyes widened. "Are you speaking of one arrogant, pig-headed, ill-mannered male in particular?"

Tayla hunched her shoulders. Damn that nectar. It was potent enough to make her say things that were better left unsaid.

"Not just one." She tried to divert her companion's sudden suspicion. "Males are all the same."

The small demon hopped off the chair, regarding her with a lift of his heavy brows.

"Not all, *ma belle*."

Oh. She grimaced. The nectar had not only loosened her tongue, it'd clearly stolen her manners.

"I don't mean you, Levet. You're completely unique," she assured him. And she didn't lump him in the same category as other males.

The gargoyle might occasionally make her a little nuts, but he was the closest thing she'd ever had to a friend.

"True," he readily agreed. "I am quite rare. But there are males who are worthy. And I am just the demon to assist you in discovering one."

"That's very kind, but I have no need for a well-meaning cupid to be interfering in my life," she swiftly assured her companion.

"Fah." Levet's wings quivered with outrage. "Cupid is a jack."

"A jack?" She struggled to decipher the Levet-speak. "You mean a hack?"

"*Oui.* What kind of love expert would shoot his victims...ah, I mean his customers...with arrows?"

Tayla couldn't halt her reluctant chuckle. He had a point. "They claim love is painful."

The gargoyle snorted. "Ridiculous. It is a beautiful magic that fills the world with joy. Which is why I will be so successful. Magic is my greatest talent."

Tayla didn't actually know if the gargoyle was going to be a success or not. So far the fire sprite hadn't returned, threatening to rip off his wings or burn down her house. That was a bonus.

But she had deliberately avoided any interest in his services.

The last thing she wanted was a love connection.

"Not that I doubt your talents, but shouldn't a love expert have a mate of his own?" she instead demanded.

He gave a flick of his tail. "Alas, I am a gargoyle who is meant to fly free."

She rolled her eyes. "Convenient."

"But we are not discussing *moi*," he continued. "I am concerned about you, *ma belle*."

"I assure you there is no need." With firm steps, Tayla crossed the kitchen, efficiently loading the dishwasher with the dirty pans. "I'm very happy with my life."

"*Non*." The gargoyle waddled to stand at her side. "You are content, but there is no happiness in those beautiful eyes."

She stilled, battling back the memories of blistering hot passion and an overwhelming need that she'd worked so hard to lock away.

"Please, Levet," she breathed.

"Were you hurt in the past?" the demon pressed. "Did a foolish male dare to break your heart?"

She shivered. "I would never be stupid enough to give my heart to anyone."

A knowing smile touched Levet's mouth. "Ah."

Enough. Tayla slammed shut the dishwasher before turning to head out of the kitchen. Maybe a long walk would banish the sensation that a dark storm was looming on the horizon.

"Save your magic for the women who hope for a true mate," she warned the gargoyle. "I can promise that I'm not interested."

"We shall see," Levet called from behind her.

Baine decided that being an ancient dragon had its benefits.

He had a ruthless power that terrified anyone foolish enough to cross his path. He could travel between worlds and was treated as a god by millions of demons. He had a hidden lair filled with his priceless hoard. And endless minions who devoted their lives to ensuring his comfort.

He was also a shape-shifter. Which meant that he could transform—from his ten-foot dragon with narrow, leathery wings and a long snout that breathed fire when he was annoyed, to any creature he wanted.

At the moment, he'd chosen a human form with a narrow face that had sculpted features and almond-shaped eyes that glowed in the firelight like the finest amber. His hair was as black as midnight and fell as smooth as satin to brush his shoulders.

As was his habit, he was wearing a pair of loose dojo pants that revealed his pale skin that was covered in tattoos. Not the usual tattoos. These strange symbols held a metallic shimmer as they crawled over his body, changing colors with a dizzying speed.

Few people realized that the symbols held the precious information he'd acquired over the endless years.

Like a portable library.

He was a dragon who understood that wealth didn't only come in gold and silver. The greatest treasure was knowledge.

Of course, he didn't ever say no to gold or silver...

Sprawled in the gilded throne that was situated on a raised dais, he gazed down the long room with ivory walls that were inset with arched mirrors. Overhead, the coved ceiling displayed a mural of Aladdin and his lamp that seemed to dance with life in the light from the exquisite Venetian chandelier, while the floor was glossed to a brilliant sheen that emphasized the inlaid ebony.

A beautiful room that was ruined by the sight of the troll with its grotesque features and large tusks protruding from his lower jaw.

He hated dealing with trolls. Who didn't? It was bad enough they were painfully stupid, but to add insult to injury, they left a stench behind that took days to scrub out of the rugs. They did, however, pay their debts.

If not always in the way Baine desired.

Wrinkling his slender nose, Baine watched as the nasty creature waved his hand toward the half-dressed females who lingered next to the arched gold-and-ivory door.

"Pretty ladies," the troll rasped. "Much, much pleasure."

"The debt wasn't for females," Baine said, lifting his slender hand to allow flames to dance over his fingers.

Trolls, like most demons, could be killed by dragon-fire.

The idiot looked confused.

"Pretty men? Me can do—"

"Gold, you moron," he interrupted the ridiculous offer. As if a dragon would need the help of a troll to find sexual partners.

Even now, the women were eyeing him with an open longing that had nothing to do with their position as concubines, and everything to do with the feral sensuality that smoldered in his amber eyes.

"The agreement of the loan was that you repay me in gold."

The pasty face paled to an ugly shade of ash. It was never wise to piss off a dragon.

"Very well."

"Wait," Baine abruptly commanded.

Yaki reluctantly turned back to eye him with a wary expression.

"What?"

"Release the females."

The troll widened his crimson eyes in shock. "Release them?"

"Do you have a hearing problem?" Baine drawled.

"No, my lord." The idiot gave a sharp clap of his hand and the smaller troll who was standing near the door hurried to unlock the iron cuffs that were used to hold the women captive. Giving a deep bow, Yaki backed out of the room. "Me go now."

Baine barely noticed the females who giggled and fluttered near the doorway. Even freed of their chains they sought to capture his attention.

Instead his focus remained locked on the troll who continued to back away. Sneaky bastard.

"You'll return with my payment."

Yaki bobbed a deep bow. "Yes, my lord."

"Soon."

"Yes, yes. Soon."

Baine waited until the bastard thought he was on the point of a clean getaway.

"And Yaki?" he murmured ever so softly.

The demon froze in fear. "Me?"

"Yes you, you dolt. If I hear you're dealing in the slave trade again I'll have you skinned and roasted for dinner." He smiled, the fire dancing over his skin. "Understood?"

"Understood," the troll choked out, no longer trying to hide his terror as he turned and trampled two women as well as his fellow troll on his way out of the door.

Baine snorted, glancing toward the tall, slender male dressed in crisp white shirt and black pants. Char was a half-breed dragon with short silver hair and eyes the color of a thunderstorm.

He'd been given to Baine on the day that Baine had left his father's lair, and the two had been inseparable since that moment nearly five hundred years ago.

Stepping from the shadows, Char efficiently rid the throne room of the females who were covertly trying to inch in Baine's direction. Once sure the intruders had been escorted back through the portal to their own world, the servant returned to study Baine with a faint smile.

"How many times must I warn them that I'm not interested in slaves?"

There was a momentary pause, as if Char was recalling a time when one particular slave had entranced Baine. Thankfully, the younger male might be irreverent, mocking, and occasionally defiant, but he was never, ever stupid.

No one mentioned the female who'd once dared to defy him.

Not even Baine's closest friend.

"Trolls have never been burdened with intelligence," Char said instead, strolling across the polished floor to stand directly in front of the throne. "And they're accustomed to dealing with your father, who still clings to the old ways."

Baine's lips twitched. His father was definitely old-school.

Pillaging, raping, scorching entire civilizations when the mood took him.

"Do I sense disapproval for my refusal to remain in the Dark Ages?" he murmured.

Char chuckled. Like Baine, he'd shrugged off the chains of the past and embraced the new world.

"The women might have been slaves, but not one of them would have said no if you'd asked them to stay."

"I don't need a troll to be my pimp," Baine growled. "I can have any woman I want."

Char cocked a brow. "Is that why your harem is empty?"

Sparks flickered over Baine's skin, his tattoos swirling until he managed to regain control over his temper.

His empty harem was yet another conversational no-no.

"Who's next?" he snapped, his voice edged with annoyance.

Usually he enjoyed collection days. What wasn't to enjoy?

There was money. Gold. Precious gems. And an occasional artifact that was worthy of his library.

But today he was feeling...odd.

As if he had an itch deep inside him that he couldn't scratch.

"Cava, King of the Rock Clan," Char answered his question, although his expression was speculative as Baine tapped his fingers on the arm of the massive throne.

"Diamonds, I suppose?" Baine muttered. The orc still owed Baine for services he'd performed nearly four hundred years ago.

Char shrugged. "It's rumored that he discovered a rare text buried in the mountains. I know how you love your musty books so I told him to bring the manuscript instead of the gems."

"Good. Send him in…" Baine's words died on his lips as he abruptly surged to his feet. "Wait."

Char was instantly at his side. "My lord?"

Baine closed his eyes, allowing his senses to rush toward the portal that had remained open.

There. He sucked in a deep breath, savoring the scent he'd been searching for, for over twenty-five years.

Tart and sweet, like lemonade on a hot summer day.

"It's her," he rasped, refusing to accept he could be mistaken. "At last."

"Is there an intruder?" Char demanded. "Shall I summon the guards?"

"No." Baine shuddered, feeling as if he was in molting season. And in a way he was. After years of frustration, he was shedding the dreary numbness that'd plagued him and replacing it with a sensation that was vibrantly sensitive to the world.

Yes. He shuddered in ecstasy. This was what it meant to be alive. If he'd been in dragon-form he would have stretched out his wings and roared in exaltation.

"There's no intruder."

Char sent him a confused frown. "Then what is it?"

"A long-lost treasure," Baine assured his companion, leaping off the dais and heading toward the nearest door.

"Where are you going?"

"Collect the debts and rid the lair of the riffraff," Baine commanded, his long strides never faltering. He was on the hunt, and nothing was going to interfere. Not this time. A sudden smile of anticipation curled his lips. "Oh, and have my harem opened."

CHAPTER TWO

It was close to midnight and Tayla was pulling her
nightgown over her head when she felt the first wave of
heat prickling over her skin.

What the heck?

Autumn in the Midwest meant chilled nights with a
brisk breeze. There was no reason she should feel as if
someone had just opened an oven.

Not bothering with a robe to cover her thin eyelet
gown, she headed barefoot down the stairs and out the
back door to her private garden.

The strange sensation couldn't be what she feared,
she silently reassured herself. Baine was in another
dimension. And even if he was in this world, she'd
hidden herself behind layers of magic.

He couldn't track her down.

It was impossible.

Right? *Right?*

Fiercely battling back the urge to panic, she glanced around the thick shadows. They were far enough from any town to ensure there were no stray lights, and Tayla was an imp, not a vampire, which meant she didn't have their ability to see in the dark.

"Levet?" she called softly, her toes curling as she hesitantly crossed the terrace that was coated in frost. "Who's there?"

For a second there was nothing but the distant howl of a coyote. Then a soft, male chuckle drifted through the air.

"As lovely as ever, imp," a dark voice mocked.

Tayla froze. *Shit.* Why hadn't she brought a flashlight with her? Or a flamethrower.

Maybe a small nuclear bomb.

She cleared the lump from her throat, a horrid sense of premonition inching down her spine as a dark shadow detached itself from near the gazebo.

"You're trespassing on private property," she said, proud when the words didn't come out as a terrified squeak. "Show yourself."

Someone, or something, gave a loud click of their tongue. "You dare to try and command me? Surely you haven't forgotten the terms of our relationship, have you, imp? I am the master, and you are my slave."

Her hand lifted to press against her heart that couldn't find a proper rhythm. It was too fast, too slow, then it forgot to beat at all. Sweat dripped down her brow and she struggled to breathe as another wave of heat threatened to smother her.

"No...this has to be a nightmare."

"Most females would consider me a fantasy come true, not a nightmare."

"Then why don't you go lurk in their gardens?"

"Because it's you that I want."

No. *No, no, no.*

She licked her dry lips. "How did you find me?"

There was another low chuckle. "Did you truly believe you could hide from me forever? You belong to me. This moment was inevitable."

Oh hell. With a surge of blind panic, Tayla was whirling on her heel and darting back into the house, pausing to close and lock the door behind her.

As if that was going to somehow keep out a full-blooded dragon.

Yeah, and she was going to sprout wings and fly to Mars.

Not. Gonna. Happen.

On the plus side, she did manage to zoom back up the stairs at a speed she would never have thought possible. Heading toward her room, she was forced to skid to halt as Levet suddenly appeared in the middle of the hallway.

"Tayla?" His eyes widened as he took in her wild hair and too-pale face. "*Ma belle*, what has happened?"

She pressed a hand to the wall as her knees threatened to give way.

Baine.

Was here.

In her garden.

After twenty-five years of hiding, he'd managed to find her.

But how?

"Did you do something?" she blurted out.

The gargoyle frowned in confusion. "*Qu'est-ce que?*"

"Your magic," she said.

Levet shook his head, giving a wave of his hand to fill the hallway with a floating ball of light.

"*Ma belle*, you're not making any sense."

She forced herself to pause and take a deep breath, trying to clear her fractured thoughts.

She wrapped her arms around her waist as she trembled with…what? Fear, certainly. Annoyance. And was that excitement? Oh, rats.

"Could your magic interfere with a disguise spell?" she demanded.

"Of course not—" Levet's startled words were cut short as his wings fluttered and his tail twitched. "Oh."

Tayla grimaced. She didn't like the sound of that 'oh.'

"What does that mean?"

Levet didn't answer. Instead he countered with his own question. "Tell me what has you so upset."

She would never have told him if she'd been in her right mind. She didn't ever talk about her past. After all, sharing could be dangerous. Not only to herself, but also to the person who she might be foolish enough to tell.

They might very well be tortured for any information of her whereabouts.

Dramatic? Maybe. But she didn't want to take any chances.

Now she found the words tumbling from her lips before she could censor them.

"Twenty-five years ago I was working at my father's jewelry store in Las Vegas when a group of trolls burst through the back door and kidnapped me."

"Trolls? In the middle of Vegas?" Levet appeared oddly confused. "That was unusually bold for the creatures."

"Not really." She shrugged, trying, as always, to block the memories of the horrid night. "They must have seen I was there alone. I couldn't have fought off one, let alone three."

Levet managed to look even more confused. "You were there alone?"

"Yes. My father had a shipment of gems coming in so he took the guards with him," she explained. At the time she'd been surprised by her father's insistence that he take the entire staff with him, but later she had to assume he must have suspected there was going to be trouble that night. "He'd only been gone a few minutes when the bastards came into the shop and tossed me into a box made of iron."

Levet hissed in anger. "I know those boxes. Only mine was silver." He shivered. "They were slavers?"

She nodded, startled by the gargoyle's confession. Clearly they had more in common than she realized.

"They weren't actually in the trade, but they supplied the..."

"Merchandise," Levet finished for her.

She shuddered. At the time she'd thought nothing could terrify her more than being hauled to a smelly camp hidden in the middle of the Mojave Desert. She'd been bathed in fine oils and dressed in a tiny bit of satin so she could be bartered off to the highest bidder.

But there was worse to come.

"Yes, but they didn't put me in the auction," she admitted. "Instead they offered me as a prize to a dragon."

"A dragon." Levet blinked. And blinked. "Do you mean a real dragon?"

Another shiver raced through her. She'd been as shocked as the gargoyle when she'd been tossed through a portal and landed in a tangled heap in the middle of a shadowed cavern. Remaining on her knees with her head bowed, Tayla had fearfully peered through her tangled hair at the lethal creature who'd studied her with a blatant hunger.

She'd immediately known it had to be a dragon even though she'd never actually seen one in person. But despite the humanoid form with thick black hair and a brutally carved face, there could be no mistaking the sizzling power that had threatened to grind her bones into dust. Or the tendrils of smoke that curled from the flared nostrils.

At the time she had no idea if he intended to eat her or force her into his bed, but without warning, another male had entered the room.

Not just a male, but another dragon, she'd swiftly realized.

This one, however, was...

Words had failed her, as she'd taken in the stark, unimaginable beauty of his lean face that had been framed by glossy black hair. His features were finely chiseled, with a hawkish nose and angular cheekbones. His brow was wide, intelligent, and his lips beautiful, but hinting at a cruelty that'd made her shiver. His eyes had been faintly slanted and smoldered with an amber fire that'd slid over her with a barely concealed contempt.

It was only when she'd unconsciously risen to her feet that his eyes had narrowed, the disapproval searing away as he'd allowed his gaze to roam down her tense body.

To Tayla, it'd felt as if she'd been struck by lightning. Her breath was wrenched from her lungs and her entire body tingled with an awareness she didn't understand.

With a slow, purposeful stride he'd crossed the cavern to stand directly in front of her. He was wearing a loose pair of linen pants that'd fallen low on his hips, revealing the mesmerizing tattoos that had moved in strange patterns over his pale skin. Halting directly in front of her, his hand had reached out to cup her chin so he could study her with a blazing intensity.

And then he'd said one word.

"Mine."

She jerked herself out of the past.

"A real dragon," she managed to choke out, wishing she could forget the absolute sense of rightness that'd filled her at his possessive claim.

"Baine."

Tayla studied the small gargoyle in shock. "You know him?"

Levet gave a dismissive wave of one clawed hand. "We have mutual friends, although we have never been formally introduced. What did the monster do to you?"

"Nothing," she said.

It was true. He had done nothing more than lean down and brush a burning kiss over her lips. But it'd felt like...everything.

She was still reeling from his touch when the older dragon had stood and shoved aside the heavy throne he'd been seated on. There had been a short but angry conversation between the two males in a language she didn't understand, although she'd managed to work out that the dragon closest to her was named Baine, and that the older dragon was his father, Synge.

While they were quarrelling a robed servant had arrived to lead her to another cavern that had been shrouded in satin curtains and finely woven rugs. "I was taken to his harem and I decided that I didn't particularly care for the role of concubine." She shrugged. "So I left."

Levet made a sound of disbelief. "You...left? And the dragon just let you?"

She wrinkled her nose. She'd been in a mindless daze when she'd been urged through curtains and into the vast room that was filled with beautiful fountains and even more beautiful women. But the second she'd realized exactly where she was, and what would be expected of her, she'd panicked.

"I didn't ask for his permission."

"*Sacrebleu*," Levet breathed. "That's impossible. No one can escape from a dragon lair."

"I was lucky. I happen to have a talent for creating portals." She licked her dry lips. Had she heard something downstairs? Was Baine already in the house? "I kept on the move for years, and then when I decided to open this teahouse I had it wrapped in disguise spells that should have kept me hidden."

A strange expression seemed to ripple over Levet's bumpy little face.

"*Oui.*" He cleared his throat. "As to that."

She frowned. "As to what?"

"Do you recall that we discussed using my magical services to discover your perfect love-match?"

"I recall telling you that I have no desire for any love-match," she said with a sharp impatience. "What does that have to do with the disguise spells?"

"It is vaguely possible that I—"

"Imp." The powerful sound of Baine's voice echoed through the air. "Enough games. Present yourself to me."

That toxic mixture of fear and excitement thundered through Tayla, draining the color from her face.

"Oh…hell," she muttered.

"I am sorry, *ma belle*," Levet told her, his wings fluttering as he moved around her to head down the hallway. "I will make him go away."

She reached to grab his shoulder. "Are you nuts?" she hissed. "You can't confront a full-blooded dragon."

"This is my fault. I must fix it."

His fault? Tayla had no idea what he meant. Levet hadn't known that she was being hunted by a pissed-off dragon.

Before she could demand an explanation, however, he was slipping from her grasp and heading toward the stairs at a surprising speed.

"Levet," she muttered, her hands clenching in frustration. Dammit.

The foolish gargoyle was going to get himself killed.

She was torn between dashing after the retreating demon to try and halt his idiotic burst of heroism, and leaping out the window so she could lead the dragon away, but the decision was taken out of her hands.

"Hello, imp." The dark, enticingly accented voice wrapped around her like a caress.

Or maybe a noose.

Stiffening, she sucked in the intoxicating scent of exotic spices and sheer male power.

She hadn't sensed him entering the house, but Baine had the sort of magic that allowed him to disguise his presence. Which meant he'd deliberately allowed her to feel his heat from the gardens. Dammit.

Now her every nerve ending screamed in response to his sudden appearance.

Accepting it was too late to flee, she slowly forced herself to turn and face the male who stood in the center of the hallway.

The breath was jerked from her body as she reacted to his sculpted beauty that really should have been illegal.

He was the most powerful creature to ever walk the earth. Why the heck did he also have to have a face that looked like it'd been carved by the hands of an angel? Or sleek black hair that had a satiny sheen as it brushed against his broad shoulders? Or eyes that burned with an amber fire?

And that body…

God almighty. Even now she found herself mesmerized by the exquisite tattoos that were crawling over his lean, sculpted torso.

Is that why he never wore more than a pair of loose pants?

Because he knew it made poor, hapless females wonder what it would feel like to run their hands over those strange markings? And kiss a path over his smooth chest and down the flat planes of his stomach? And tumble him onto the floor so she could climb on top of him and...

Slamming the mental door on her vivid fantasies, Tayla fiercely reminded herself that she was in trouble.

Ass-deep-potential-death kind of trouble.

"How did you get in here?" she demanded.

He shrugged, taking a slow, thorough survey of her. Tayla shivered. There was a smoldering intensity in his gaze that seemed to singe her skin. She didn't know what was going on behind those painfully gorgeous features, but she sensed it was raw and needy and possessive as hell.

Christ. It was true.

Dragons truly did lust over their hoard.

"The fey are not the only ones who can create portals," he warned, his eyes at last lifting to meet her wary glare. "Give me your name."

"It's none of your—" Baine's power thundered through the air, cutting off any urge to be a smartass. "Tayla," she choked out. "My name is Tayla."

"Tayla." He said it slow. Like he was testing it on his tongue. Then he gave a slow nod. "Yes."

"Did..." She was forced to halt and clear her throat. "Did your father send you?"

He seemed surprised by her question. "Why would you think Synge would send me?"

"The trolls—"

"My father has no claim on you," he interrupted in fierce tones. "I paid for you. Now you belong to me."

"What do you mean, you paid for me?"

"The usual." He shrugged. "He demanded a small fortune, and I gave it to him. Let's hope you're worth it."

"No," she breathed, her heart thundering at the mere thought of belonging to this intensely beautiful creature.

There was a long, nerve-racking silence as he did another slow, ruthless survey of her tense body, as if satisfying himself that his prize hadn't been damaged or tarnished over the years. Then, without warning, he reached out to grasp her wrist in a grip that sent shockwaves of heated pleasure through her.

"Time to go home."

She barely managed to gasp before the world melted to black.

Baine deliberately chose to return to his home through the portal that opened just outside his lair. He still didn't know how she'd escaped his father's harem, but he could only assume that someone had been foolish enough to leave a gateway open.

This portal was constantly guarded, which meant she couldn't use it to sneak away.

Still holding her arm, he stepped through the opening, waving aside the uniformed guards who snapped to attention.

"Welcome home, my lord," one of the soldiers murmured, his gaze running an appreciative inventory over the lovely imp at Baine's side.

Baine narrowed his eyes, acutely aware that Tayla was wearing nothing more than a tiny scrap of clothing that did nothing to hide her beauty. His power abruptly vibrated through the air. He was a dragon. Which meant nobody was allowed to covet his treasures.

Especially not this one.

"Open the door," he snapped.

There was a flurry of movement as his servant scurried to obey his command and within seconds Baine was tugging Tayla into his lair. Even then, he continued through the long hallway, not halting until they'd entered the empty throne room.

Alone at last.

His gaze swept down her body with a compulsive fascination he couldn't seem to halt. It was pissing him off. He'd already assured himself she was undamaged. And that she wasn't carrying any weapons. Not that there was anything she could possess that would hurt him. But she might try to harm his guards, or even herself.

There was no need to keep inspecting her as if he'd been starving for the sight of her. Or for his hand to twitch with the need to reach out and assure himself that she was real. Or suck in deep breaths just so he could savor her tart, lemony scent.

It'd been the same way the first time he'd caught sight of her.

He'd been summoned to his father's lair to explain once again why he wasn't out pillaging and looting to fill the family coffers like his brothers. The last thing he'd expected was to be sucker-punched by the sight of a half-naked imp standing in the middle of the dank cavern.

But that was exactly what'd happened.

In that moment, the world had faded until nothing was left but the beautiful creature with a cloud of dark gold hair and wide green eyes that seemed to hold a captivating innocence.

He should have walked away. There were millions of beautiful women. All of them capable of stirring his cock without making him feel as if he suddenly discovered the reason his heart was supposed to beat.

Instead he'd walked forward and blatantly claimed her.

Of course his father, Synge, hadn't been happy. The imp had been protection payment from the trolls. Synge didn't share. Not with anyone.

By the time he'd managed to barter for the female, she'd been led away by a servant and managed to disappear.

He'd still had to pay his father three chests of gold and a priceless emerald.

Which was why he'd been so ruthlessly determined to find the elusive imp. He'd bought her fair and square. She belonged to him.

At least, that's what he'd told himself.

Now he sensed that it was far more complicated. Or maybe it was exquisitely simple. He wanted this imp more than he'd ever wanted another female in all his long, long life.

And she wanted him.

He could catch the luscious scent of her arousal the instant he'd touched her cheek, but for some odd reason she refused to accept that she belonged to him.

Even now he could sense her inner struggle to ignore the heat that smoldered between them.

"I see you're still a bully," she muttered.

"Bully?"

"Tyrant. Tormentor. Intimidator," she clarified.

He cocked a brow, his hand lifting to brush down the bare line of her shoulder, his fingers tingling at the feel of her soft, satin skin.

"If I were a bully you would already be beaten black and blue," he pointed out, his fingers drifting down to trace the plunging neckline of her nightgown. His inner fires flamed with a hunger he intended to sate very, very soon. "Instead, that pale, perfect skin doesn't have a mark on it."

She shivered as he lightly caressed the upper curves of her breasts, the jade in her eyes shimmering in the torchlight.

"You intruded into my home and kidnapped me," she said, her voice breathy. "Only a bully would do that to an innocent woman."

Baine barely listened to her foolish accusations. He didn't want to talk. He wanted…her.

Every golden, satin inch of her.

In his bed. Against the wall. In his treasure room, surrounded by precious gems.

"But you're not an innocent woman, are you, Tayla?" he murmured in absent tones. He was far more interested in the hardening nubs of her nipples he could see beneath the eyelet material of her gown.

He felt her tense. "What's that supposed to mean?"

"I bought you from my father. That means you're my property," he bluntly reminded her.

She shook her head, her heart thundering loud enough he could hear the frantic beats.

"People can't be property."

"Do you deny that your father bartered you to pay his debts?"

She jerked as if he'd actually struck her. "What did you say?"

He stilled, sensing that she wasn't faking her shock. "Your father made a contract with the trolls."

Her face drained of color, leaving it a strange shade of ash.

"My…father?" she rasped, knocking aside his hand. "What are you talking about?"

Baine scowled. He wanted to touch her.

The soft feel of her body beneath his fingertips was satisfying an ache that had plagued him for twenty-five years.

But he hadn't missed the burst of confused fear that had darkened her eyes. This female was unaware of what her father had been willing to do to save his own skin.

The knowledge was...welcomed, he abruptly decided.

First off, it helped to soften a portion of the anger he harbored toward her. He didn't like the thought that she was so lacking in integrity that she would run away from her obligation.

It also solved one of his nagging problems.

Baine might be enormously powerful, but he was also sly, and cunning, and quite capable of using his intelligence rather than brute strength to achieve his goals.

"You didn't know?" he asked in smooth tones.

"There's nothing to know." She wrapped her arms around her waist in an unconsciously defensive motion. "I was working late one night in my father's shop and the trolls burst in from the back door and kidnapped me."

"Trolls don't randomly enter public buildings to snatch females," he pointed out. "They were there to collect the only thing of value that your father still possessed."

"That's a lie," she hissed. "My father was a successful businessman who—"

"Your father was a compulsive gambler." He overrode her fierce denial.

She winced. "In the past, but he stopped when he opened the store. He promised."

"Promises from a gambler are worth about as much as gold from a goblin," Baine retorted.

She grimaced. Everyone knew that goblins could make dross look like gold. Only a fool would accept a coin from the deceitful demons.

"How would you know?"

Baine wasn't about to admit that he'd spent years discovering every possible thing about her. From the fact that her mother had died when she was just a child, to the fact that she loved to bake. He knew that she had once dreamed of owning her own business and that she started working when she was barely more than a child to support her worthless father.

Instead, he moved toward a table that was set beside the throne dais. Reaching out he tapped the top of a rosewood box inlaid with gold. A second later he flipped open the lid.

The box was magically connected to his vast library and was capable of transporting any book, manuscript, or item he might desire.

Sticking his hand into the box he grasped the scroll and turned back to Tayla. Then walking back, he halted directly in front of her and unrolled the fragile parchment.

"Is that your father's signature?" He pointed toward the name scrawled at the bottom of the page.

Even in the torchlight it was obviously written in blood. Which meant it couldn't be forged.

Tayla leaned forward, her brows drawn together in a baffled frown. "What is this?"

"The agreement made between your father and Skragg, the King of the Mojave Mountain Trolls."

She sucked in a sharp breath, her angry denial slowly being replaced with something that might have been fear as she scanned the neat rows of numbers until she reached the total at the very bottom of the parchment.

"This can't be right," she at last muttered, ridiculously determined to deny what was staring her in the face. "Even if my father was gambling, there's no way he could be in debt for over a hundred thousand dollars."

Baine shrugged. "The trolls have a reputation for extorting outrageous interest rates from their victims. Which is why only the very stupid, or very desperate, would choose to borrow money from them."

"Okay." She licked her lips, her shoulders hunched. "If my father owed this Skragg money he could have used the gems from the store to pay him off."

"He did," Baine informed her, a strange sensation suddenly twisting his gut.

He didn't like the way her eyes were darkening with hurt. Or how her body was trembling. But she needed to know the truth, didn't she?

If she understood that she had no right to run from him then he wouldn't have to keep her as his prisoner. His finger moved toward the number at the center of the page.

"This is the amount owed after he'd promised the contents of his store. When the gems were gone, he had nothing left of value to offer." He captured and held her wary gaze. "Nothing except you."

CHAPTER THREE

Tayla felt as if she'd been slammed headfirst into a brick wall.

It'd been horrible to think she'd been a random victim of the trolls. And that a ruthless dragon was hunting her.

But this…

This was so much worse.

Granted, imps tended to be flighty, self-indulgent creatures by nature, and if she was honest with herself, her father, Odel, took selfishness to a whole new level. Which no doubt explained why her older brothers had washed their hands of Odel when they were old enough to leave the nest.

But to offer her to slavers just to pay his gambling debts was inconceivable.

"I can't believe this," she breathed.

"Believe, my pretty imp. It's all written in black and white." He deliberately paused. "And blood."

She dipped down her head, unable to meet the burning amber gaze. She didn't want to accept she truly was this arrogant dragon's property. And she most especially didn't want him witnessing her increasing sense of humiliation.

"He promised," she stupidly muttered.

Baine leaned forward, whispering directly in her ear. "Do you admit the contract is real?"

She trembled, that dangerous, melty sensation she'd never felt with anyone but this male flowing through her body.

"Do I have a choice?" she muttered.

His lips brushed an erotic spot just below her jaw. Or maybe the heat of his lips made every spot on her body an erotic spot.

Dangerous, dangerous, dangerous...

"And that the trolls in good faith gave you to my father, and that it was within my right to purchase you?"

"I never agreed to become your concubine," she argued in husky tones.

"Fine." His mouth seared a path down the curve of her neck. "Then the debt must be repaid."

She swayed, exquisite darts of pleasure shooting through her as he released a small burst of power that branded her skin where his lips lingered.

It should have hurt—she didn't doubt that his dragon-fire had singed her neck. But instead she grew damp between her legs.

Oh dear goddess.

What was wrong with her?

"I can't pay it all," she breathed in desperation. "At least not right now. But I have money—"

"Not you." He jerked his head up, his elegant features suddenly hard. "The debt is your father's and only he can pay it."

"I don't know how to contact him," she muttered.

It was true. She'd deliberately avoided him after her escape, worried they would use him to try and get to her.

What a joke. All this time she'd been trying to protect him when he'd happily used her as collateral.

Baine studied her with arrogant satisfaction. "Then you belong to me."

Lifting his hand, he released a burst of fire that nearly blinded her. Then, allowing it to recede, he revealed a delicate golden chain.

A dragon marque.

Panic raced through her as he calmly slipped the necklace over her head, the precious metal warm as it settled against her bare skin.

The golden chain might be exquisitely crafted, but it wasn't just a pretty bauble. It was a visible claim that she belonged to Blaine. And no one, not even she, could remove it.

"No."

His head once again lowered, his lips only intensifying her panic as he traced the line of her jaw. His touch was light, but it ignited tiny bursts of excitement. How could she be terrified and furious and aroused all at the same time?

"Yes," he murmured.

"Baine."

His mouth scorched the curve of her throat, the brush of his dragon-fire making her shudder.

"I like the sound of my name on your lips."

The urge to whisper his name again and again was nearly irresistible. *Crappity, crap, crap.*

"If you will just give me time I can pay you back—"

Her words were cut short as he covered her mouth in a kiss that demanded complete and utter surrender.

"I have waited twenty-five years," he at last whispered against her throbbing lips. "The debt will be paid now."

Without warning Tayla felt herself being swept off her feet and carried toward one of the double doors located behind the throne.

"Where are you taking me?" she demanded, not surprised when the words came out as a squeak.

"To the harem," he informed her, stepping through the door and into a long corridor lined with priceless tapestries. "Where else?"

Where else, indeed.

Trembling as he pressed her tight against his chest, she studied his starkly beautiful face as he easily carried her down a long flight of stairs.

A voice in the back of her mind continued to screech out a warning. She needed to flee. This dragon was dangerous. And not just because he could turn her into a crispy critter.

The first time she'd encountered Baine she'd told herself her fierce response to his beauty was a result of her weakened state.

She'd been kidnapped, terrorized, and tossed through a portal into a dragon's lair.

Any female would be a little sensitive.

But now she couldn't pretend her reaction was anything but the result of a female screamingly attracted to a gorgeous, sensual male. She had to get away before her treacherous desires made her do something she was going to regret.

But even as the urge to flee pulsed through her body, there was another part of her mind that whispered she wasn't being fair.

How could she leave?

As much as she might hate it, her father had given her as payment. The debt might be Odel's, but he'd paid it by selling his only daughter.

Wasn't she being as dishonorable as her father by trying to escape?

Trapped in her dark thoughts, she barely noticed her surroundings until Baine came to a halt and slowly lowered her to her feet. Taking a step away from the sizzling heat of his body, she glanced around the vast courtyard with a large fountain in the center of the smooth paving stones.

Overhead was a honeycomb dome that allowed in a golden patchwork of sunlight. Illusion? Probably, but it felt real. The floors were tiled into a beautiful mosaic of blue and yellow and brilliant red, and the windows covered by delicate lattice panels. There were bronze urns that stood taller than her and chandeliers crusted with breathtaking gems.

At the far end of the courtyard were arched doors that led to the private rooms where she could catch glimpses of low, deeply cushioned sofas and oversized velvet pillows. No doubt the rooms were filled with beautiful women who devoted their lives to pleasing their master.

As far as prisons went, it wasn't bad.

She wrinkled her nose, her gaze lingering on the fountain that sprayed a sparkling cascade of water into the air. Okay. It was better than 'not bad.' It was as close to paradise as she'd ever been.

But that didn't make it any less a prison.

She heaved a wistful sigh, unprepared for Baine to grasp her chin and tug her face up to meet his brooding gaze.

"Don't," he commanded in abrupt tones.

Tayla frowned. "Don't what?"

"Look so hurt," he growled, his amber eyes smoldering with frustration. "It...troubles me."

"It troubles you?" she demanded. Was he serious? Did he expect her to be dancing with joy? "What about me? I just learned that my own father bartered me off like a piece of property."

He studied her, his fingers skimming lightly down her throat to linger on the small, sensitive burn he'd created with his dragon-kiss.

"Do you fear your time with me?" he asked, something in his dark voice suggesting he wasn't pleased by the thought she might be afraid of him. "I have no intention of hurting you."

Weirdly, she believed him. His touch was possessive, but oh-so-tender. As if he was deliberately leashing his power to make sure he didn't bruise her skin.

She shivered. *Bad Tayla.* She wasn't supposed to be thinking about his soft caresses. Or imagining those slender fingers stroking down her naked body while he gently parted her legs and...

"That's not the point," she abruptly muttered. *Yeesh.* This dragon was obviously screwing with her mind.

He toyed with the tiny ribbon that was threaded through the neckline of her nightgown, the back of his fingers brushing over the upper curve of her breasts.

Sparks crackled over her skin.

"Then what is?" he demanded.

She struggled to remember. She had a point. Of course she did. It was just that it was hard to think when her nipples were hard.

"I have a life. A business," she at last managed to latch on to a stray reason. "I don't want to be a part of your harem."

###

Baine made a sound of annoyance. Why was she making this so difficult?

She should appreciate the fact that he'd brought her to his harem that had been specifically designed for her comfort. And that he'd treated her with such fragile care.

It wasn't as if she didn't share his desire. Her arousal scented the air like the finest perfume.

Torn between the need to carry her to the nearest bed and prove her reluctance was no more than a pretense, and his pride that demanded she admit the truth without his coercion, Baine stiffened as Char whispered in the back of his mind.

Dammit.

What now?

"Choose your bedroom and change into one of the gowns," he commanded, sweeping an arrogant hand toward the arched doorway. "I will return to share our dinner."

Without warning, the imp reached out to grasp his arm.

"Baine," she said in a soft protest.

His gaze was locked on the fingers that lay against his bare skin. They were slender and pale and exquisitely feminine in contrast to the vivid tattoos that swirled over his body.

It was the first time she'd willingly touched him. The sensation was...cataclysmic.

"You've accepted you belong to me," he said, the words clipped. He wasn't prepared for her to witness his intense reaction.

There was a pause before she gave a grudging nod of her head.

"Yes."

"Then do as I command."

Shaking off her hand, he turned to head out of the courtyard. He'd reached the door when her voice brought him to a sharp halt.

"How long?" she demanded.

He glanced over his shoulder, feeling a funny twinge in the center of his chest at the sight of her standing alone in the middle of the room. With her shoulders squared and her chin tilted to a proud angle, she should have looked silly. He could destroy her with one puff of fire.

But he'd never seen anything more beautiful.

Her hair tumbled down her back, shimmering with hidden hints of golden fire in the sunlight that streamed through the dome. Her eyes were the color of the purest emeralds with shards of jade. And her slender body was visible beneath the thin fabric of her nightgown.

"What?"

"How long am I to remain your prisoner?"

He scowled. Aggravating imp.

For centuries he'd enjoyed females who eagerly competed to enter his bed. A few had killed for the privilege. So why did this imp pretend it was a punishment to be his lover?

"You're my courtesan, not my prisoner," he informed her. "And you'll stay with me until I say you may leave."

Her lips thinned. "In other words, I'm your prisoner."

"You're very stubborn."

"Not stubborn, merely weary of having my life screwed up by males who think they own me."

Baine made a sound of impatience, resuming his exit out of the courtyard.

"Prepare for my return," he ordered in tones that left no room for argument.

He was heading up the stairs when he heard the sound of shattering glass. Tayla had just destroyed one of his priceless urns. Without warning, his lips twitched. Then he tilted back his head to laugh with rich enjoyment.

He hoped it was the orange one with gaudy opals that he'd received as a gift from an ancient aunt.

He hated that thing.

Refusing to dwell on his strange, unpredictable responses to the female, he instead focused on the slender male standing on the top step.

"Char," he murmured, coming to a halt directly in front of his servant. "Maybe I didn't make it clear I had no desire to be interrupted."

The male grimaced, his eyes darkened to smoke. "You made it clear, but we have a problem."

Baine was on instant alert. "Tell me."

"Your father."

"What about him?"

"He just arrived."

What the hell? Baine momentarily froze. He couldn't have been more shocked if Char had told him that the tooth fairy had magically appeared.

Then, with a shake of his head, he was heading toward his throne room, his long strides eating up the distance.

"Did he give a reason for his visit?"

Char hurried to keep pace, his expression grim. "No, but he brought gifts."

"Damn." Baine's initial shock was quickly replaced with suspicion as he sent his companion a warning glance. "Put the guards on alert."

Char instinctively reached to touch his dagger with the diamond blade that he had strapped beneath his shirt.

"You expect trouble?"

Baine clenched his teeth. "When my father arrives bearing gifts, he intends to try and bribe me into doing something I don't want to do. Or…"

"Or?" Char prompted.

"It's a declaration of war."

Shoving open the door, Baine stepped into the throne room. Heat immediately blasted around him. Even braced for his father's power it made him flinch.

Synge was a large, cruel, lethally clever predator. Currently he'd chosen a human form with dark hair that he kept cut short and eyes the color of polished silver. Striding up and down the length of the room, he was dressed in leather pants and a black T-shirt that looked as if it'd been painted on his broad chest.

He had tattoos similar to Baine's, although not nearly as many and they didn't swirl. Instead they faded in and out, sometimes disappearing for days.

Synge preferred brute strength to intelligence. He'd never been a collector of knowledge.

Remaining close to the door, Baine waited for his father to halt his pacing and turn to face him before he performed a small bow.

"Sire."

The older man moved toward him, his broad, roughly carved face impossible to read.

"Baine."

"To what do I owe the honor?"

Halting a few feet away, Synge cocked a dark brow. "Can't a father visit his son?"

Baine gave a sharp laugh. His father had kicked him out of the family lair the second he was old enough to be considered a threat. Synge didn't share. Not his harem, not his power, and certainly not his hoard.

And while the older male had occasionally commanded Baine to return home so he could inform

Baine of his severe disappointment in his eldest son, Synge had never once stepped foot in Baine's lair.

"He could, but in five hundred years you've never bothered to visit before, so you will understand my surprise," Baine drawled.

Synge folded his arms over his chest, a nasty smile curving his lips.

"And you claim I have no manners."

Baine shrugged. He didn't know why his father was there, and frankly he didn't give a shit. His only interest was returning to the female who he'd waited twenty-five years to bed.

"I'm too busy for games," he said in cold tones.

"So I've heard," his father drawled.

Baine stiffened. A nasty premonition crawled through him, twisting his gut into a tight knot.

"What did you hear?" he demanded.

"That you have my pretty little imp."

Shit. Why hadn't he realized that his father's sudden appearance was connected to Tayla? There were no such things as coincidences.

But he was truly caught off guard.

Ruthlessly leashing the aggression that detonated through him at the mere thought that another male was interested in his female, he clenched his hands into tight fists.

"Who told you?"

"It doesn't matter." The T-shirt nearly split in two as Synge deliberately flexed his muscles. "I want her."

"No."

Danger vibrated through the air. No one said 'no' to Synge.

"The trolls gave her to me."

"And I bought her."

Synge waved a hand toward the heavy trunk that was sitting on Baine's throne.

"I'm returning your payment."

Baine forced himself to suck in a deep breath. Christ. His every instinct urged him to attack.

It didn't matter that this dragon was his father. Or that Synge was offering a fortune for the imp's return. His primitive nature only knew that another male was trying to take away his female.

Once he'd stifled his more violent urges, his brain came back online, allowing him to consider his father's unexpected arrival with a much-needed logic.

The first question was how the hell Synge had discovered he'd managed to locate Tayla. It had to be a spy in his household, of course. Nothing else would explain how the older dragon had learned about her presence so quickly.

Dragon-fire licked over his skin. He would deal with the traitor later.

For now he was much more interested in discovering his father's interest in Tayla. It had to be a significant reason for him to return a fortune in gold and an emerald the size of a baseball.

"Why?" he demanded.

Synge abruptly turned to pace toward the far wall, pretending an interest in a marble statue that was set in a shallow alcove.

"I want the imp," he said.

Baine's brows snapped together. His father wasn't subtle or devious or capable of elaborate schemes. He was a bully who was blunt to the point of rudeness.

So what was he hiding?

"For what purpose?" he pressed.

"The same purpose I want any female." Synge turned to face him, a ruddy color staining his face. "To warm my bed."

He was lying.

The question was…why?

"If that was true then you would chose a concubine from your harem," Baine pointed out. "You have no need to pay for a bed-warmer."

Synge glanced toward the treasure chest on the throne. "You were willing to pay."

Baine shook his head. "Tell me why you want her."

A low growl rumbled in his father's chest. "She's a beautiful creature and she lingered in my thoughts after she…" There was the slightest pause. "Disappeared."

Baine stepped forward, the air prickling with his power. "I don't believe you."

"I've returned your payment," Synge snarled, his belligerent tone intended to intimidate. "Now give me the imp."

"No."

Tension pulsed in the air, the potential for a bloody confrontation a tangible force.

Then, with an obvious effort, Synge dialed back his hostility.

"So you're my son after all," he jeered. "Fine. You want more treasure? I'm prepared to barter."

It was so out of character for his father to even suggest he negotiate rather than simply take what he wanted that Baine should have shouted with joy.

How often had he wished he could see his father groveling at his feet?

Instead, all logical thought was shattered as the beast inside Baine roared, his skin suddenly feeling too tight for the fury that pounded through him.

Barter for Tayla?

Not a chance in hell.

"She's not for sale," he rasped.

The silver eyes burned with a strange desperation. "Of course she is." Synge stepped forward, the words that Baine never thought to hear tumbling from his lips. "Name your price."

Baine couldn't concentrate on his father's bizarre behavior. Not until he'd made certain the bastard understood there was no way he was getting his hands on Tayla.

"There's nothing you could offer that would tempt me." The throne room trembled from the force of his anger. "She's mine."

Synge stepped forward, his hands clenched into tight fists.

"I've tried to do this the easy way, Baine, but I will have that imp one way or another."

Baine whirled on his heel and headed toward the exit. He needed to be with Tayla. To assure himself that his treasure hadn't been stolen while he was being distracted.

"As far as I'm concerned this conversation is done," he informed his father.

"Don't be a fool, Baine," Synge warned. "You stand in my way and I'll destroy you."

Baine never hesitated. Yanking open the door, he motioned for his waiting servant.

"Char, my father is leaving." He headed directly for the stairs. "Make sure he doesn't return."

CHAPTER FOUR

Tayla was pacing the courtyard when she heard the sound of approaching footsteps.

Baine.

A shiver of anticipation raced over her skin.

It'd been less than half an hour since she'd seen him, but her body was reacting as if it'd been waiting a lifetime to once again feel the brush of his dragon-fire.

The realization pissed her off.

She didn't want to be aroused by the impossibly beautiful creature. Not when he was responsible for destroying her life.

Okay. That wasn't entirely fair. Her father was ultimately responsible for the whole destroying life thing, but still…Baine was the one holding her captive, right?

Squashing the tingly awareness that fluttered in the pit of her stomach, she watched him stride toward her with an inhuman grace.

If she hadn't been distracted by her unwelcomed response, Tayla might have noticed his grim expression and the frantic swirl of his tattoos as he halted directly in front of her.

Instead, she fiercely stoked the flames of her temper, ready for battle.

"We need to…" His snarly words trailed away as his gaze lowered to her nightgown. "Why haven't you changed?"

She sent him a narrow-eyed glare. She'd done a quick inspection of her new home while he was gone, astonished by the subtle elegance of the various rooms. Where was the tacky strip-club vibe she'd expected in a harem?

She'd been even more astonished to realize she was completely alone. There hadn't been one sign that there was another female living in the vast complex.

Not until she'd opened the closets to discover dozens of gauzy gowns meant to entice a male.

The mere thought of wearing clothing that belonged to Baine's lovers made her shudder in revulsion.

"I don't wear other women's cast-offs."

He scowled. "What makes you think they belong to some other female?"

She wrinkled her nose. "They smell like…"

"What?"

"Perfume," she admitted.

"Ah." Unexpectedly, Baine's features eased, almost as if he was pleased by her words. "And the thought of my other concubines troubles you?"

Yeah. Not going there.

She would have her tongue yanked out before she admitted that his other females bothered her.

"I want my own clothes."

His hand reached to trace the ribbon running along the neckline of her gown.

"The gowns were brought here for you," he murmured. "No other female has touched them."

"Oh." She faltered. The gowns belonged to her. That seemed...dangerously thoughtful. She bit her bottom lip, her heart pounding as his fingers brushed the upper curve of her breast. Crap. She was going to be melting into a puddle of goo if she wasn't careful. "I still prefer my own clothes," she forced herself to choke out.

The amber eyes smoldered with a wicked invitation. "Why?"

Why? She had a reason. Several perfectly logical reasons.

If only she could think of them.

She cleared the lump from her throat, fiercely forcing herself to concentrate on the fact that she was nothing more than a possession to this male. A part of a dragon hoard, to be used and then tossed aside when a new, shinier treasure appeared.

"You've forced me to leave my home, my business, and my friends," she managed to point out. "I want something that's mine."

He studied her stubborn expression, no doubt wondering why he'd been so eager to bring her to his harem.

"Are you always so difficult?" he at last demanded.

"If you want an obedient slave then you should choose some other woman from your harem."

The amber eyes blazed with a tangle of emotions.

Possession. Need. A confusing hint of wariness.

"I've chosen you," he informed her.

"Lucky me," she muttered, telling herself that his words didn't make her tremble with pleasure.

Not that she managed to fool herself.

Or the dragon who smiled with smug male satisfaction as he felt her tiny tremor.

"True," he agreed, wrapping one arm around her waist to pull her against the searing heat of his body. Then, tangling his fingers in her hair, he tugged her head back to meet his hungry gaze. "You're very fortunate that I am willing to ignore your ridiculous pretense that you don't want to be my concubine."

Her mouth went dry, her body softening as it molded against his hard muscles. Her pride, however, instantly rebelled at his egotistical assumption that he was irresistible.

He was, of course. But she wasn't going to admit it.

"Are you delusional?" she groused.

Baine flattened his hand against her lower back, pressing her against the hard thrust of his arousal.

"I'm honest, which is more than you can claim, my sweet Tayla."

Her stomach clenched, a throbbing emptiness pulsing low in her body.

She wanted to wrap her legs around his waist and feel that large cock slowly sinking deep inside her. She wanted his lips pressed to her throat, singeing her with his dragon-kisses.

The vivid images slammed into her with shocking force.

Yeesh. It'd clearly been way too long since she'd had a lover. Now she was panting with her brutal need.

"Don't," she muttered, her hands lifting to land against his chest.

He pressed his face into the curve of her neck, sucking in a deep breath.

"I can smell your desire." His fingers tightened in her hair. "It's a fragrance that has haunted me for twenty-five years."

Panic jolted through her. What was wrong with her? She was supposed to be enduring his touch with contemptuous resignation, wasn't she?

After all, he could demand the use of her body, but her pride needed the pretense that it was completely against her will.

Instead she was melting like a spineless sex slave.

"Because you're using some weird dragon-magic on me," she accused in desperation.

He lifted his head, regarding her with a confused frown. "Dragon-magic?"

"Don't pretend you can't make females desire you."

He blinked, then with a soft chuckle he lowered his head and resumed his destructive path of kisses down the length of her throat.

"I can," he admitted without a smidgeon of modesty. "But it has nothing to do with magic."

His tongue touched the pulse pounding at the base of her neck and Tayla squeezed shut her eyes. Oh...damn. She didn't want to listen to her pride. She wanted to melt beneath the golden pleasure flowing through her like warm honey.

"Baine," she breathed.

He planted bold kisses over the upper curve of her breasts. "Say it again," he commanded.

"Baine," she muttered, not because he ordered her to say his name. Heck, no. It just happened to be the only word she was capable of forming as his lips traced the deep vee of her neckline.

Her nails dug into his chest, her hips instinctively pressing forward. With nothing but two thin layers of fabric between them, she could feel the perfect outline of his cock as he rubbed it against her lower stomach.

One tug on those loose dojo pants and she could have her fingers wrapped around his erection and—

The fantasy had barely started to form when it was rudely interrupted when Baine muttered a low curse and reluctantly lifted his head to study her with a brooding gaze.

"We can't finish this here," he growled. "We have to go."

She blinked. *Go?* Her body was trembling with need and he wanted to leave?

"Go where?" she rasped.

"This lair is no longer safe."

Oh. She gave a slow shake of her head, trying to concentrate on his warning. What on earth could make a dragon's lair unsafe?

A horde of demons? An outbreak of Ebola? An invasion of space aliens?

None of them seemed likely.

"What does that mean?"

His fingers brushed her cheek before he was stepping back. "That's a question only you can answer."

"Me?"

Before she could demand an explanation for his cryptic accusation, Baine was grasping her wrist. Whispering a word of power, he opened a portal and tugged her through.

Baine stepped out of the portal, his lips still carrying the taste of tart lemon and warm, willing woman.

It was...

He struggled to think of the appropriate word.

Aggravating, he at last decided.

He understood lust. And the need to safeguard his treasures. He was a dragon. It was as natural as breathing. But this overwhelming need to touch and hold and protect this female was becoming an obsession that consumed his every thought.

If he was smart, he would cut his losses and walk away.

There were a million women to fill his harems. All of them capable of slaking his lust without disrupting his well-organized life.

But even as a voice in the back of his mind whispered to release Tayla and return to his lair, he was grasping her elbow even tighter as they stepped out of the portal.

This woman belonged to him. It didn't matter what he had to do, or who he had to kill—he was going to keep her.

Almost as if sensing the intensity of his emotions, Tayla shivered, her eyes widening as she caught sight of the large house shrouded in darkness.

"You brought me home?" she breathed, her lips curving.

He shrugged, his chest tightening at the sight of that smile. "You said you wanted your belongings."

Without warning, she tugged free of his grip and hurried toward the wide porch.

"I—"

She made a strangled sound as he caught her arm and yanked her to a halt. Dammit. He'd been so preoccupied by this female, he'd completely missed the danger waiting for them.

Idiot.

"Wait, Tayla," he snapped.

He felt the second she caught sight of the front door that'd been ripped off the hinges and the window that was broken.

"What have you done?" she demanded in tragic tones.

Baine bristled, instantly offended. He'd treated her with the utmost care. How dare she imply he would vandalize her home like a common thug?

"Why would you assume this is my work?"

"You're my only enemy."

"I am not your enemy—" He broke off the ridiculous argument as the scent of granite filled the air.

Turning his head he watched as a miniature gargoyle rounded the side of the house and hurried directly toward Tayla.

"Ah, *ma belle*," the odd creature called out, his large wings flapping in agitation. "Have you been harmed?"

Tayla appeared annoyingly happy to see the gargoyle. "I'm fine."

"Thank the gods. I have been so—" The gargoyle gave a startled squeak as Baine grabbed him by one stunted horn and lifted him off his feet. "Eek."

Baine frowned. He recognized that smell. The stunted demon had recently been in the company of the vampires who'd sought his assistance.

So why was he in Tayla's home? And more importantly, why did he assume he could treat her with such familiarity?

No male, no matter how tiny, was allowed to touch his female.

"Who are you?" he snarled.

The gargoyle gave a snap of his wings. "I am the mighty Levet. No doubt you have heard of me."

"No." He allowed his fire to dance over his skin. A tangible warning of the lethal flames he could conjure with one breath. "You will pay for what you've done."

Tayla reached out to lay a restraining hand on his arm. Immediately he quenched his fire. The flames wouldn't hurt her, but her skin was so delicate he wouldn't risk even the smallest mark.

Unless it was his dragon marque, he silently reminded himself. He was fiercely pleased that she wore the golden chain that would warn every male that she was claimed.

"Baine, don't," she pleaded.

He scowled at the gargoyle who called himself Levet. "This creature has dared to damage your property."

"*Moi?*" The gargoyle wrinkled his tiny snout. "Why would I garbage my own home?"

Baine frowned. What the hell?

"Trash," Tayla corrected him, "It's trash your house." She turned her attention to Baine. "Release him."

Baine experienced an odd pang in the center of his chest. "You share your home with this...thing?"

"Hey," Levet squawked.

"He is demon with feelings, not a thing," Tayla protested. "And he's my friend."

Her fierce defense of the gargoyle did nothing to ease Baine's annoyance.

He continued to glare at the creature. "Why are you so small?"

Levet's tail tangled around his clawed feet that dangled off the ground.

"I am not small. I am pleasingly compact."

Baine narrowed his gaze. "Hmm."

Tayla made a sound of impatience, stepping so she could study the gargoyle's ugly face.

"What happened?"

"I was attempting to find a means of rescuing you when a pack of trolls barged into the house," Levet told her.

Baine abruptly dropped the gargoyle, his attention locked on the house.

First his father was demanding Tayla's return. And now trolls?

It couldn't be a coincidence.

Tayla pressed a hand to her chest, as if the sight of the damage was physically painful.

"Why would they tear up my house?" she breathed.

Levet moved to stand at Tayla's side. "I think they were looking for something."

"Looking for what?"

"You."

"Oh." She bit her bottom lip, her eyes darkening to jade in the fading moonlight. "I always feared they wanted to punish me for escaping," she whispered, glancing toward him with a vulnerability that made his gut clench. "Do you think that's why they were here?"

He didn't have a fucking clue, but he would rip apart the world to track them down and destroy them.

"We need to collect your belongings and leave this place."

"You think they'll return?"

He gave a slow dip of his head. "Now that they have your scent I think it's a distinct possibility."

"How did they get my scent in the first place?" Her brows abruptly snapped together. "For that matter, how did you? I have the house layered with spells that should have protected me."

Baine shrugged even as Levet cleared his throat. "As to that—"

"Later," Baine interrupted. He didn't have time to worry about the reasons her spells had failed. The only thing that mattered was taking her someplace where he could make sure she was safe. "We can't linger here."

"Bossy," Tayla muttered, moving to head up the stairs and through the open door.

Baine remained at her side. He'd already used his acute senses to assure himself that there was no one else in the house, but he intended to make sure there were no traps left behind by the trolls.

He didn't trust the sneaky bastards.

In silence they moved through the house that seemed to be stuffed with an overabundance of flowery furniture and lacy doilies. Baine felt a burst of fury at the sight of several knickknacks that had been broken, and the nasty stench of troll that marred the warm scent of freshly baked bread.

This had been Tayla's lair.

A cozy home where she'd felt at peace.

He would obliterate every damned troll who'd dared to invade her space.

Tayla climbed the stairs to the second floor and headed to the last door at the end of the hall.

Anticipating the opportunity to catch a glimpse of the female's most private sanctuary, Baine nearly ran her over when she came to abrupt halt and reached through the doorway to grab a suitcase that was clearly sitting at the edge of the entrance.

He frowned in confusion, reaching to take the case. "Were you planning on leaving?"

She shrugged, her expression suddenly unreadable. "I've been on the run for years. I'm always prepared to leave."

Baine narrowed his gaze, sensing a wound that had festered for years.

He didn't need to ask who'd caused her injury.

Her worthless father.

Reaching out, he cupped her chin in his palm and tilted back her head.

"You won't leave me," he said, the words a stark warning. "Never again."

Her eyes sparked with an annoyance that banished her pain. Baine hid a smile. This was how he wanted to see her. Vibrant, strong, and ready to fight him despite the fact it would forever be a losing battle.

Her lips parted but before she could speak, the idiotic gargoyle waddled down the hallway, his polished tail trailing behind him.

"Where are we going?" the strange creature demanded.

"You're not going anywhere," Baine snapped. "At least not with us."

The gargoyle gave a flap of his wings. "But—"

"Go away," Baine commanded.

Tayla turned to face him. "I want to speak with Levet in private."

The beast inside him snarled with fury. It didn't matter that Levet was a stunted creature who was clearly no match for a full-grown dragon. Or that Tayla claimed they were friends.

He didn't want any male near his female.

"It's too dangerous," he chided. "We need to be away from here."

"It will only take a minute." She held his gaze, forcing herself to say the magic word. "Please."

Baine swallowed a curse.

He could easily compel her to go with him. With one burst of power could open a portal and have her pulled through before she could protest.

So why didn't he?

That question didn't have an easy answer.

"You have five minutes," he snapped, pointing a warning finger at the gargoyle. "You touch her and I'll rip off your wings."

With his warning delivered he headed down the stairs, carrying Tayla's suitcase.

Just like he was some damned bellboy, he realized in disgruntled   disbelief.

CHAPTER FIVE

Tayla watched as Baine grudgingly headed down the stairs.

She hadn't actually expected him to give her the time she'd requested. Baine was a dragon who gave orders; he didn't take them. Now she sucked in a deep breath.

Blessed goddess. Being near Baine was like standing in the center of an electrical storm. She felt scorched from head to toe.

And not in a bad way.

"A little possessive, is he not?" Levet murmured.

Tayla shrugged, feeling a blush touch her cheeks at Levet's speculative gaze.

"He's a dragon and he believes I'm a part of his hoard," she said.

"And that's all?"

It was, of course. Even if a small part of her wished...

No. She wasn't going to go there.

Not ever.

"Isn't that enough?" she demanded.

"Perhaps."

She gave a shake of her head. She didn't want to discuss the fact that she was nothing more than dragon booty.

"Look, I'm sorry, but I'm going to be gone for a while," she confessed. "If you don't fear the trolls then you're welcome to continue your dating service here."

Levet gave an offended sniff. "I fear no trolls."

"Good." She allowed a wry smile to touch her lips. She truly was going to miss this tiny demon. "I'd like to think you were here to take care of the house."

"*Non*," he protested, his wings flapping. "I am going to find a means of rescuing you from that unpleasantly rude dragon."

She was shaking her head before he finished speaking. "It's impossible."

"Fah." He gave a wave of one clawed hand. "Impossible is not a word I comprehend, *ma belle*. Have I not told you that I am a certified KISA?"

Tayla frowned. She'd become fairly proficient in Levet-speak, but this was a new one.

"KISA?"

"Knight In Shining Armor."

Ah. Of course. She swallowed a small chuckle.

"I don't doubt your...skills, but this is a matter of honor. I have to stay with Baine until he choses to release me."

"I do not understand."

"My father, Odel, owed the trolls money," she reluctantly admitted. "A lot of money."

"So...*mon dieu*." Levet's tail snapped around his feet as he realized what she was saying. "It is your father's debt to pay," he protested.

She felt a familiar stab of resignation. Odel was an expert in screwing up his life and expecting someone else to suffer the consequences.

"He paid it with me."

"You are saying Odor—"

"Odel," she corrected.

"Odel," Levet muttered in disgust. "He used you to settle his gambling debts?"

She gave a reluctant nod. "Yes."

Levet's wings drooped. "Please do not do this, *ma belle*."

As if she had a choice?

Tayla abruptly grimaced. Dammit. There were few things she hated more than those who wallowed in self-pity.

She'd made the decision to honor the debt.

She wasn't going to moan and groan about it now.

"I have to go. I'll return as soon as I can."

She reached out to gently touch one of the stunted horns before she headed down the stairs. Following the tiny shockwaves of power that pulsed through the air, she found Baine waiting for her on the porch, her suitcase in one hand.

On the point of joining him, her feet came to an abrupt halt as she caught sight of the tiny figurine that'd been busted when the trolls had forced their way into her home.

With a sound of distress, she bent to gently gather the shattered pieces off the floor.

It wasn't a masterpiece. In fact, it was a cheap trinket from some fairy celebration. But it was one of her mother's few possessions that her father hadn't sold over the years.

Which made it priceless to her.

There was a brush of warm air wrapping around her before Baine was standing at her side, his voice unexpectedly gentle.

"It can be repaired."

"I suppose," she muttered, setting the pieces on a nearby table.

She would deal with the destruction later.

Straightening, Tayla was caught off guard when Baine brushed his fingers over her cheek, capturing a stray tear that she didn't even know was sliding down her face.

"You seem...sad," he accused, his voice rough as if angered by her emotional reaction.

Tayla sniffed, her gaze moving to the door that was hanging at a drunken angle.

"I should have known better than to try and create a home," she muttered, talking more to herself than the dragon studying her with a brooding gaze. "Every time I do it only leads to disappointment."

His fingers aimlessly drifted to outline her lips. "Your father didn't provide you with a nest?"

She gave a lift of her shoulder. "He tried on occasion, but he spent most of our time on the run from his bookies."

His touch heated against her skin, as if he was struggling to contain his dragon-fire.

"Worthless creature."

"It doesn't matter." She squared her shoulders. Hadn't she just promised herself she wasn't going to give in to self-pity? "Not any more."

"You're under my protection now," he growled, grasping her chin to tilt back her head. His amber gaze scorched over her face with blatant possession. "Unlike your father, I will always make sure you're safe."

She shivered. But it wasn't fear.

No. The delicious tremors were in direct response to the strong arms that were abruptly wrapping around her to tug her against his hard, half-naked body.

"Even from yourself?" she breathed.

His arms tightened as his head lowered. "I cherish my treasures," he assured her, his lips skimming over her forehead, then down the length of her nose.

A groan was wrenched from her throat as his hands cupped her backside and he tugged her tight against his thickening cock. His lips brushed her cheeks, then over her mouth before skimming the length of her jaw.

Each tiny caress set off a series of sparks that raced through her with dizzying pleasure.

Mmm.

Her fingers landed on the bare skin of his chest and treacherous desire curled through the pit of her stomach. He was heat and raw male power.

She didn't know if he actually cherished her, but he certainly knew how to make her smolder with need.

Dragon-magic...

His clever mouth explored along the line of her throat, searing the skin over her racing pulse before heading down to the curve of her breasts.

"Baine," she choked out as her nipples tightened to painful nubs and moisture gathered between her legs.

She wanted to use the tip of her tongue to trace every fascinating tattoo that danced over his skin. She wanted to skim her hands over the chiseled muscles that made him look as if he'd been sculpted by an artist. She wanted him to lift her onto the nearby table. To spread her legs so he could step between them and ease the unbearable ache.

But even as the X-rated fantasies flared through her mind, she was forcing herself to remember that Levet was upstairs and they were standing in the middle of an open doorway.

With a satisfying groan, Baine was lifting his head, staring down at her with a brooding gaze.

"You're right," he muttered, a startling color blooming along the line of his prominent cheekbones. "This is not the place."

She studied his beautiful face as he wrapped his fingers around her wrist and made a slashing motion with his free hand.

Was he embarrassed?

That seemed...unlikely.

Baine was one of the most lethally gorgeous creatures to ever walk the earth. Women no doubt tossed themselves at his feet. Not to mention the fact that he had harems filled with countless courtesans.

Why would he be bothered by a few kisses?

She on the other hand, had every reason to be shamed by her response. The man was her captor. He was forcing her to become his concubine.

It didn't seem right to be considering how quickly she could get him naked so she could finish what he'd started.

A thick darkness surrounded them as Baine tugged her into his waiting portal, then, without warning, they were stepping into bright sunlight.

She blinked, lifting her hand to shade her eyes as she took in their new surroundings. Her breath locked in her lungs.

It was magnificent.

Truly magnificent.

In a daze, she allowed her gaze to take in the rolling meadows filled with wildflowers that danced on the slight breeze. In the distance she could see the silhouette of mountains capped with snow, and the sparkle of sunlight reflecting off a nearby lake. But it was the small cottage with a thatched roof that was directly in front of her that captured and held her attention.

It was perfect.

Painted a pristine white with green shutters, it was framed with daisies and pretty pink tulips. A flagstone pathway led from the terraced porch toward the narrow road where Tayla was standing. Heck, it even had a picket fence.

It screamed 'Home' with a capital H.

"What is this place?" she breathed.

Baine stood at her side. Close enough to wrap her in his comforting heat, but not touching her.

A shame.

No. Bad Tayla, she silently chastised herself. There was no lusting over the yummy dragon.

"Your fantasy," he answered, his dark brows arching as a blush stained her cheeks.

Damn. He couldn't read her fantasies, could he?

"Mine?" she squeaked.

"My magic will conform our surroundings to the desires of my guests."

She blinked, her attention returning to the cottage. He was right. It was like something out of her dreams. The quaint sort of place where an imp could live in peace.

"It's an illusion?" She couldn't hide her faint pang of disappointment.

"No. It's real." He stepped forward to push open the gate that was bordered by roses. "Just a matter of perception."

Okay. That made sense. Sort of.

"But where are we?" she pressed.

"We're hidden between dimensions." He glanced around, as if as if to make sure they were alone. "No one should be able to track us here."

His assurance reminded her of their abrupt departure.

"Why did we have to leave your lair?"

"A story for later." With a hypnotizing grace, he turned and without warning scooped her off her feet and cradled her against his chest. His very bare, very lickable chest. "You're tired," he announced.

She shivered. She was never going to get used to the electric tingles that raced through her when this male was near.

"Are you asking me or telling me?" she demanded in wry tones.

He carried her up the flagstone pathway and onto the porch. "I can sense your weariness."

On cue her head dropped against his chest, her muscles aching.

She had no idea what time it was, but it felt like an eternity since she'd been slipping on her nightgown and preparing for bed.

"It's been a long night," she conceded in weary tones.

"Yes."

There was a strange tingle in the air, then abruptly the sun disappeared and they were standing beneath a velvet black sky spangled with distant stars.

Holy crap.

"That's quite a trick," she muttered, impressed in spite of herself.

"It's only one of many," he smugly claimed, lowering his head to halt her response with his dragon-kisses.

A good thing.

She fully intended to tell him that he was an arrogant ass.

Instead, she signed beneath the melting pleasure of his kiss as the exhaustion she'd been battling for the past few hours slowly won the war.

Unlike many mongrels, Craven could pass as human.

His face was square with bluntly carved features, and his blond hair was buzzed close to his skull.

True, he stood nearly seven foot tall, and had thick slabs of muscles that meant he had to have his T-shirts and jeans custom tailored. And his eyes flashed crimson when he was pissed off. Which was most of the time.

But most people assumed he was one of those steroid-crazed gym addicts who wore his wraparound sunglasses 24/7 because he thought it made him look cool.

Idiots.

For years he'd lived among them, being tutored by his mother in the art of black magic. She'd devoted her life to training him to kill the monsters who'd captured her when she was barely more than a child, and raped her. The fact that Craven was a product of that violent encounter only made the thought of revenge all the more sweet for his mother.

Craven had agreed.

Besides the powerful magic, he devoted himself to honing his fighting skills. By the time he was in his early twenties he was proficient in killing with every known weapon, not to mention his bare hands.

He was a lethal assassin who stalked the demons and destroyed them without mercy.

It wasn't until his mother's death that he'd doubted his ruthless quest.

As much as he enjoyed hunting demons, it didn't exactly pay the bills. What human agency was willing to pay for the very fine troll head collection he had mounted on his wall? Hell, humans didn't even realize they were mere cattle being stalked by predators that lurked in the shadows.

That's when he'd made the decision to organize a small band of fellow half-breeds who had skills similar to his own, and began hiring out their services to the highest bidder.

Assassins, who would kill anyone or anything for the right price.

It was a well-paying gig, but still Craven wasn't satisfied.

He wanted the big score. The one that would allow him to retire and live in the luxury he intended to become accustomed to.

It was a dream that had been destined to remain unfulfilled until twenty years ago when his top lieutenant, Reece, overheard a drunken troll bragging that he knew how to sneak into a dragon's hoard.

Craven wasn't stupid. He knew there was a good possibility the troll was blowing smoke out his ass. It was common knowledge that trolls liked to brag. But if there was even an off chance that the demon was telling the truth, it was worth the bother of kidnapping the creature.

Unfortunately, Skragg had proved to be a less than successful partner-in-crime. The troll claimed he knew of an imp who could help them, but so far he hadn't managed to produce the elusive fey. The only thing he'd been able to offer was a few strands of the imp's hair that Craven had used to cast his scrying spell.

Over the years, Craven had nearly forgotten about the damned thing. Until the spell had abruptly activated the day before.

Now he stood at the top of the stone staircase of the abandoned castle on the Norwegian-Swedish border, looking down at the troll who had just entered the great hall along with Craven's lieutenant, Reece.

The large beast lumbered forward, his naked body covered by a thick brown skin and his features even more grotesque than most of his brethren. He had large tusks that protruded from his lower jaw and crimson eyes that shimmered in the torches that lined the paneled walls.

Reece, on the other hand, was a slender male who was half-fairy. He had long black hair that he kept pulled from his narrow face in a long braid. His features were delicate, which might have caused trouble among Craven's rough and ready gang of outlaws if it wasn't for the cold glitter in the green eyes.

Reece could kill as easily he breathed. And often did.

He also provided the portals the assassins used to travel around the world.

Keeping his gaze locked on the troll who came to an awkward halt at the bottom of the stairs, Craven planted his hands on his hips.

"Skragg," he said, his eyes narrowing. "Where's the female?"

The troll gave a shake of his massive head. "She no there."

"Impossible," Craven snapped. "The spell was triggered."

"She no there," Skragg repeated.

Trolls. Fluent in zero languages.

He turned to study his lieutenant who was shivering in the crisp morning air despite his long leather jacket. His fey blood preferred warm weather.

"Reece?" he demanded.

"Our incoherent friend is right," the fairy said, his expression hard with frustration. "The imp had disappeared by the time we reached her house."

Craven muttered a foul curse. He'd waited twenty years to get his hands on the imp and these two idiots had walked away just because she wasn't in the first place they searched?

"Why the fuck didn't you follow her trail?" he snapped.

"She left through a portal," Reece said. "It was impossible to track her."

Well, damn.

"Do you believe she will return?"

The younger male shrugged. "I suspect the house is her current lair."

"Then you will keep a watch on the place until she returns," he instantly commanded.

It was a waste of Reece's considerable talents to be stuck on a mindless stakeout, especially since they didn't have a clue where the female had gone or when she would return.

But there was no way in hell he was going to risk losing the opportunity to get his hands on a dragon hoard.

Surprisingly, Reece grimaced. "That might be difficult."

"Why?"

"She doesn't live alone."

"Another imp?"

"No, a gargoyle."

Craven blinked. He'd heard of the gargoyles, of course. But like any demon with a functioning brain, he did everything in his power to avoid them.

"What interest does the Guild have in the female?"

Reece gave a lift of his hands. "Impossible to say. There was also the smell of a dragon in the house."

"Dammit." Annoyance transformed into fear. Surely fate wouldn't be so cruel as to dangle the treasure in front of his eyes and then snatch it away at the last second? "Does he have the female?"

"No Synge," the troll grunted. "Baine."

"Baine?" Craven gave a frustrated shake of his head. "What the hell is he bleating about?"

"Skragg claims that Synge is the dragon who first owned the imp, and that Baine is his son," Reece explained.

Craven scowled. Like that was supposed to be better?

"Are they be working together?"

Skragg made a slashing motion with his hand. "No like."

Craven shook his head. He might have troll blood, but he'd spent the majority of his life trying to kill the bastards, not communicate with them.

It was Reece who once again translated.

"Skragg is convinced that the father and son aren't exactly friendly," the fairy said.

"So he intends to use the imp to betray his father?"

Reece shrugged. "Or to barter for a portion of his treasure."

Craven abruptly slammed his fist against the heavy wooden bannister, indifferent to the dust that drifted down from the open-beamed ceiling.

"We need to find her," he snarled.

Reece gave a sharp laugh. "If I could open a portal into a dragon's lair we wouldn't need the imp."

"Then we have to find a way to lure the dragon out of his lair," Craven announced, his tone warning he wasn't going to tolerate failure. "I want that imp and nothing is going to stop me."

CHAPTER SIX

Baine carried the sleeping Tayla into a room at the side of the cottage and settled her in the middle of the bed. Then, tugging the quilt over her slender body, he simply stood there and studied her delicate features.

There was no reason to linger.

She was in a place where she could be protected. And it would be several hours before she would waken so she could offer him the pleasure he'd waited so long to enjoy.

It was clearly an irrational waste of time to watch as her silky golden hair spread over the pillows. And her lush lips parted as she released a small sigh.

But even as he urged his feet to carry him out of the cottage, he found himself unable to resist the desire to simply savor the sight of her lying in his bed.

How many nights had he fantasized about this moment?

More than he wanted to admit.

A raw jolt of satisfaction raced through him.

She was where she belonged.

At last.

He remained standing beside the bed for several more minutes before he at last forced himself to head out of the cottage so he could open a portal to his lair. Standing at the entrance, he called for Char to join him.

It took less than five minutes for the younger male to step out of the portal and glance around his surroundings with a lift of his brows.

"This is..." His lips twitched as he glanced toward the small cottage and picket fence. "Quaint."

Baine ignored his companion's humor. If the cottage pleased Tayla then that was all that mattered.

"I want you to stand guard."

Char returned his attention to Baine. "You think the imp will try to escape?"

Did he?

Baine hesitated before giving a sharp shake of his head. Unlike his private lair, this temporary bubble between dimensions wasn't magically protected to prevent portals. But while Tayla had the magic to leave if she wanted, he trusted that she wouldn't try to escape.

Unlike her spineless father, Tayla had a sense of honor.

She wouldn't flee until he released her from her debt.

Something he had no intention of doing for the next several centuries.

Perhaps never...

"No, she won't try to leave," he said. "But I won't allow her to be unprotected."

Char instinctively glanced around the empty meadows. "She's in danger?"

"She's being hunted and I want to know why."

The gray eyes narrowed. Char possessed a shrewd intelligence that was one of many reasons he was Baine's closest companion.

"Does this have anything to do with your father's visit?"

"He demanded that I give him Tayla," Baine admitted, an ugly anger twisting his gut. Just saying the words made him want to release his flames and destroy anything that might be a threat to his female. Suddenly he understood his ancient ancestors' habit of causing massive destruction. "In fact, he warned me that he would stop at nothing to get his hands on her."

Char frowned. "Did he say why?"

"No." Baine planted his fists on his hips, tiny tendrils of smoke swirling around him as he struggled to leash his fierce anger. "But I suspect it's the same reason the trolls want her."

"Trolls?" Char gave a choked cough. "Is that a joke?"

Baine cocked a brow. "Do I ever joke?"

"Ah…" Char cleared his throat. "No."

"Keep her safe."

With his warning delivered, Baine turned toward the portal only to come to a halt as Char laid a restraining hand on his shoulder.

"Wait, Baine," he commanded. "You aren't going to confront your father, are you?"

"Not yet." Fire danced over his skin, hot enough to make Char take a hasty step backward. "First I have a traitor to uncover."

Continuing through the portal, Baine entered his lair and headed directly toward his throne room. Along the way he sent out a mental command for his servants to join him.

He wasn't a cruel master. Unlike most dragons, he was firm but fair with his staff. He found that offering respect to his people earned him far greater devotion and loyalty than trying to intimidate them with fear.

Now it pissed him off to realize he'd been betrayed.

Settling on the throne, Baine watched in silence as the various servants crowded into the long room. There were half-breed dragons, along with Weres who made up his personal guards. Then there were the flighty fey who were his household servants, and the dozen vampires who tracked down demons who owed him payment for services rendered.

Bloodsuckers were the ultimate debt collectors.

Waiting until they were all on their knees with their heads bowed, he at last spoke.

"One among you has betrayed me."

Shock reverberated through the room like a mini earthquake.

Baine filled the air with the heavy weight of his power, not halting until he heard the distressed whimpers from the fey.

"Confess and I will make your death swift." Baine deliberately paused, carefully watching the various demons as they kneeled before him. "Make me waste my time to discover the truth and I will destroy you so slowly you will plead for death."

There was a long, fear-drenched silence before one of his soldiers grimly rose to his feet.

Baine felt a stab of shock as he realized that it was Fist, one of his favorite guards. Damn. It was bad enough to be betrayed without it being someone he actually liked.

"M-my lord—"

"Stop," Baine growled, halting the stumbling words as he waved a hand toward the rest of his servants. "Out."

Waiting until the crowd had hastened out of the room, Baine used his magic to block the door before he turned his attention back to Fist.

"Now, speak."

The half-breed dragon lowered his head that had been shaved bald, his large body trembling.

"I plead for a quick end," he rasped.

"Look at me." Baine didn't try to stifle the fire that continued to flicker over his skin or the curls of smoke that wrapped around his feet.

Fist swayed, his face paling to a pasty white as he forced himself to lift his head and meet Baine's furious glare.

"My lord."

"Tell me why," Baine snarled.

"Your father holds my mate captive."

The simple words slammed into Baine with unexpected force.

Just a few days ago he might have dismissed the explanation as a meaningless excuse. How could a mate be more important than a male's pledge to his master?

Now, he had the sudden thought of what he would do if someone were holding Tayla hostage.

The answer came without hesitation.

He would destroy the world.

Several worlds.

Not that she was his mate... Of course not.

He gave a shake of his head, forcing away the inane thoughts. Right now all that mattered was discovering why the hell his father would have planted a spy among his servants.

"How long?"

"Twenty-five years."

Baine surged to his feet. He *knew* it.

All of this came back to Tayla.

"Tell me exactly what my father wanted from you."

"He said you were searching for a female imp," Fist admitted, flinching as Baine's fury blasted through the air, shattering the chandeliers. "I was commanded to let him know when you located her."

Baine stepped off the dais, moving to stand directly in front of Fist.

"Why?"

Fist lifted an unconscious hand to wipe the sweat that was dripping from his brow.

"He claimed that she had information he wanted."

Baine paused, sorting through his memories of the night Tayla had been offered to his father.

He'd sensed his father's lust for the beautiful imp. What male wouldn't want to bed her? But the older dragon hadn't revealed an interest in anything more than adding her to his large harem. Hell, he'd readily agreed to hand her over to Baine once he'd bartered for an outrageous price.

If she had information he needed, why not hide her away in his dungeons where he could force her to talk?

"Did he say what information?" he demanded of Fist, not surprised when the soldier gave a shake of his head.

"No."

Of course he hadn't. Synge might be a brute, but he wasn't stupid.

Still, Baine sensed that Fist had noticed something. "No, but...?"

Fist grimaced. "I had the feeling he was worried."

"About the imp?"

"About the information she possesses."

Baine turned to blindly stare at the statues that lined the walls. A greedy Synge was dangerous.

A frightened Synge was lethal.

"Damn," he muttered. What the hell was going on?

Absently he paced from one end of the room to the other.

What information could Tayla possess that was a threat to Synge?

Did it have something to do with her father? Or had she heard something or seen something while she was in his lair?

Lost in his dark thoughts, it took a moment for him to hear Fist's soft plea.

"My lord."

He turned to study his companion with an impatient frown. "What?"

"I know I don't deserve your mercy, but I fear what your father might do to my mate if he discovers that I confessed I am the traitor," Fist admitted, his voice raw with a fear that came from his very soul. "Could you make my death appear to be an accident?"

"You aren't going to die," Baine snapped. The male would have to pay for his betrayal, but Baine wasn't a mindless savage. He understood that destruction wasn't always the best solution. Fist might very well be of use in the future. "At least not today."

Fist was intelligent enough to realize there was a reason he wasn't already burnt to a tiny cinder.

"What do you want from me?" he demanded.

"I want you to contact my father."

"Why?"

Baine considered for a long moment. Synge hadn't survived for thousands of years by being lazy. There was no way he was going to simply give up if he truly wanted Tayla.

Even now, the cunning old brute was no doubt plotting a way to steal her from Baine.

Clearly, Baine would have to find some way to keep the older male distracted until he could figure out what information Tayla supposedly possessed.

"Tell him you overheard me setting up an auction for the female, with the trolls," he at last commanded.

Fist widened his eyes. "Trolls?"

"Yes." Baine gave a nod, abruptly heading toward the door. He was suddenly anxious to be back with Tayla. Just the thought of some male wanting to take her away from him... *Fuck.* "Tell my father that I intend to start negotiations after I've tired of her sweet charms."

That should keep his father distracted. At least long enough for Baine to find the trolls and discover why everyone was so interested in his female.

"And that's all?"

Baine ignored his companion's confusion. "For now."

"Very well."

Baine hesitated at the door, turning to glance over his shoulder.

"Fist."

The younger male tensed. "Yes?"

"After you contact my father you will remain locked in the dungeons until I decide your fate."

The soldier gave a deep bow. "Yes, my lord."

Unwilling to waste any more time on the traitor, Baine left the throne room. He would send one of his guards to escort the male to the dungeons.

He had a more important task that needed his personal attention.

The sooner it was done, the sooner he could return to Tayla.

###

Levet knew that most people thought that he was as flighty and unpredictable as a dew fairy. It didn't bother him. Who wanted to be a boring old demon who was obsessed with responsibility?

Life was meant to be fun.

But there were occasions when he could be as tenacious as a pure-blooded Were on the hunt.

Which was why he'd devoted the past four nights to searching every seedy safe house that catered to demons who preferred to remain off the radar.

Tonight he was in a dark, miserably damp street in London. This particular establishment tended to cater to vampires, but he was running out of places to search. And worse, the wood sprite he'd hired to create portals for his travels was becoming increasingly drunk on the nectar that Levet had offered as payment for his services. If the idiot passed out, Levet needed to be someplace where he could spend the day in a secure location.

Thankfully, he was BFFs with the current vampire clan chief of London. He was certain Victor would be happy to have him as a guest.

Okay, maybe not happy, he grudgingly conceded. But Victor's beautiful mate, Juliet, would insist he be allowed into their lair.

Leaving the drunken sprite seated beneath a lamppost, Levet headed down the steps that led to the cellar beneath the silent pub. Then, stepping into the large room with wood plank floors and a low, open-beamed ceiling, he glanced toward the shadowed booths that lined the walls.

He barely noticed the pathetic humans who were hidden in the shadows, their eyes glazed with drugs and their thin bodies stripped down to reveal whatever unmarred skin they still possessed. If they wanted to be a midnight snack for a vampire, that was their business.

He waddled toward the back of the room, where a male imp was wiping down the long bar. Then, with a flap of his wings, he lifted himself off the ground to perch on one of the empty stools.

Glancing in Levet's direction, the imp twisted his handsome features into a predictable sneer. With his long golden hair pulled from his narrow face and his slender body encased in skin-tight leather, he was as beautiful as most fey, but there was a nasty glint in his green eyes.

"Whadda you want?"

Levet leaned forward, keeping his voice low. "I'm searching for an imp."

"No imps, but I have a fairy who will rock your world." The man nodded toward a narrow door carved into the paneling. "Two hundred bucks plus tips."

Levet quivered with outrage. "Do I appear to need to purchase my females?"

"Hell yeah." The green eyes flicked over him with blatant disgust, a sudden greed glinting in the emerald depths. "In fact, I'm gonna have to charge you double."

The imp was clearly demented, Levet decided. That was the only explanation for his inability to see that he was a chicken magnet. Or was it chick magnet?

Whatever.

"*Mon dieu*," Levet muttered, forced to point out the obvious. "I am the world-famous Levet. Women adore me."

"Yeah, right," the imp mocked. "Sunny will adore you for four hundred dollars plus tips."

Levet made a sound of annoyance. Arguing with the idiot was clearly a waste of his time.

"The imp I seek is a male."

"Ah, why didn't you say so?" the barkeep shrugged. "I have that flavor as well."

"Fah." Enough was enough. With a flap of his wings, Levet was leaping off the stool and making his way toward the arched doorway that led into the private rooms.

"Hey." The imp was in immediate pursuit. "What the bloody hell do you think you're doing?"

"I need to search your fine establishment," Levet informed him.

"You can't do that." Moving to stand directly in Levet's path, the imp released a shrill scream when Levet gave a wave of his hand and set the buffoon's hair on fire. "Holy shit," he wailed, rushing toward the sink behind the bar to douse his smoldering curls.

"Do you wish to have another taste of my mighty magic?" Levet demanded when the imp at last straightened to glare at him.

He paled, flinching as Levet raised his hand, sparks dancing off his claws.

"No."

"A wise choice."

Strolling out of the room, Levet waited until he was in a narrow hallway before he hastily scurried forward. The imp wouldn't be intimidated for long. In fact, he was probably already calling for backup.

Passing the fighting pits that were currently empty, as well as the open cubbies for those demons who didn't need privacy for their sex, he began pushing open doors in the hopes of stumbling across Tayla's father.

Hey, it could happen.

He was at the end of the hallway when he stepped into the last room. Instantly he was confronted by a pretty fairy with a halo of golden curls and big, china blue eyes that regarded him with a wary fear. Swiftly she was trying to disguise her terror behind a forced smile.

"Hello."

"Oh. *Pardon*." Levet performed a small bow, allowing his tail to curl around his feet. He didn't want her to miss how shiny it was in the dim candlelight. "I did not intend to disturb your privacy."

"That's okay." Her slender hands fluttered down her gossamer gown that revealed her naked body beneath. "Are you my next customer?"

"*Non*." Levet closed the door and stepped forward. He hadn't forgotten his goal to locate Odel, but his instinct to play the role of Knight In Shining Armor was too compelling to resist. "You are a…"

"Whore?" she bluntly said the word Levet had been attempting to avoid. "Yes."

Levet took another step forward, glancing around the barren room that held nothing beyond a bed and narrow dresser. There were no pictures, no flowers, no hint of the usual female gewgaws that turned a space into a home. "Forgive me, *ma belle*, but are you being held against your will?"

"I…" The blue gaze darted toward the corner of the room, where a tiny red light was blinking. A hidden camera stuck in the paneling. How…clichéd. "No, of course not," the fairy continued.

Levet resisted the urge to roll his eyes. Instead he turned so he could spread his wings far enough to block the view.

"Is there more than one camera?"

She gave a tiny shake of her head. "No."

"Can they hear what we're saying?"

"I don't think so."

"*Bon*." Keeping his wings spread, Levet reached out to gently grasp the female's hand. "What's your name?"

"Sunny."

"Sunny." He gave her fingers a squeeze. "Where is your family?"

She bit her bottom lip. "They came to this place in an effort to hide from a vampire who was hunting my younger brother for trying to seduce his mate."

Levet grimaced. It wasn't an uncommon story. Fairy males tried to bed every female that crossed their paths. Regardless of whether or not she might be claimed by a possessive mate.

"You bartered yourself to pay the bill?"

"Yes."

"Do you wish to escape?"

She sucked in a shocked breath. "It's impossible."

"Nothing is impossible for me," he assured the delicate female. It was obvious the poor creature was traumatized. But why wouldn't she be? No doubt her family had left her behind when the danger from the vampire had passed, accepting that it would be her duty to sell her body in this seedy pub. "I am a certified Knight In Shining Armor."

"I..." The fairy blinked, and blinked again. "I see."

"Not yet. But you will," Levet assured her, pressing a light kiss to her chilled fingers. "First I need your assistance."

Without warning, the fairy heaved a resigned sigh. "Of course. What do you desire?"

"Not what you are imagining," he softly chastised. Releasing her fingers, he gave a wave of his hand, creating the image of Odel he'd found in Tayla's picture album. "Have you seen this imp?"

"Oh." A flush touched the female's cheeks as she leaned down to study the fuzzy face that was floating in midair. Without warning, she made a small sound of surprise. "I have."

Levet's tail twitched around his feet. *At last.*

"He was here?"

"Yes." The fairy gave a firm nod. "I saw him in the pub room last night."

"Where are the vaults?" he asked, referring to the rooms demons rented when they wanted to avoid attention.

"If they discover I helped you—"

"No one will discover you helped," he interrupted. It would take very little for the fairy to work herself into a panic.

Not that he would usually mind. A fairy in full hysteria was eager to be comforted. And he had a number of very fine techniques for calming a beautiful fey. But right now it was more important that he locate Odel. It was the only way to save Tayla from the dragon.

"You can't be sure," she breathed.

"I promise."

"How?"

He gave a lift of his hands. "I swear no matter what happens I will come back to rescue you."

Hope briefly shimmered in the impossibly blue eyes before Sunny was sending a fearful glance toward the camera.

"That's impossible," she whispered.

"What did I say about that word, *ma belle*?" he scolded in light tones. Then, giving a wave of his hand to dispel the image of Odel, he squared his shoulders. He was running out of time. "Tell me how to find the vaults."

There was the faintest hesitation before Sunny leaned down to whisper directly in his ear.

"Take the back stairs to the basement," she said. "In the last cell there's a door hidden behind an illusion of a brick wall."

"Ah." Levet gave her a cheek a small pat. "Illusions are my specialty." Turning, he headed toward the door, pausing to send her a reassuring smile. "I will return for you."

She rolled her eyes. "Right."

"I do not make promises I do not keep," he swore, stepping out of the room before those big blue eyes could lure him into forgetting the reason he was at the nasty pub.

First he had to get Odel.

Then, he would come back for Sunny.

And then...well, perhaps he would play cupid for himself and allow Sunny to enjoy the attentions of a genuine Prince Charming, aka Levet.

Tayla wasn't sure how long she slept.

It felt like several hours, but time between dimensions always flowed at its own pace. It could be a few minutes or several weeks since she'd entered the cottage. And since night and day were clearly controlled by Baine, she couldn't even use the hint of dawn that was cresting the horizon to assume it was morning.

Still, she felt deliciously rested for the first time in years, she decided. Which was all that mattered.

Scooting off the bed, she shoved her tangled hair out of her face and followed the thundering male power that hummed in the air.

"Hello?" she called out, moving through the cozy living room filled with overstuffed furniture and tiny tables covered in knickknacks.

She briefly hesitated, easily imagining herself seated in front of the fireplace, sipping tea and... She gave a sharp shake of her head. Was she nuts? Sipping tea in a dragon's lair?

She was clearly suffering from some strange Stockholm syndrome.

Forcing her feet to carry her out the front door, she glanced around the seemingly empty yard with a small frown.

"Baine?"

There was the sound of rustling leaves, then without warning a slender form was leaping from the nearby tree to stand directly in front of her.

"He isn't here."

She sucked in a startled breath, her wide gaze taking in the stranger's short silver hair and storm-gray eyes. The male was gorgeous, but she wasn't fooled by his boyish smile or the casual khakis and gray cashmere sweater.

He didn't have the same power as Baine, but he was a lethal predator who could crush her before she could hope to escape.

"Who are you?" she demanded, taking a discreet step backward.

He folded his arms over his chest, studying her with a blatant curiosity.

"Char." He performed a small bow. "Baine's most trusted servant."

A delicious heat wrapped around her, prickling over her skin like an intimate caress. *Yow.* If Baine hadn't already bewitched her with his magic she would have melted into a puddle of gooey lust.

"You're a dragon?" she demanded.

"Half-breed."

Ah. That would explain why his power had seemed muted.

It didn't, however, explain why he was in the private lair Baine had created.

"Why are you here?"

"I was commanded to protect you."

"Protect me." Tayla frowned. That didn't sound good. "Protect me from what?"

Char shrugged. "Baine was a little vague on details. Something about trolls."

Could the trolls follow her here? It seemed unlikely. So was there some other reason he was worried for her safety?

Or did he assume she was going to try and escape?

Of course. That had to be it.

The thought was somehow disappointing.

"Where did Baine go?" she asked, stiffening as Char slowly circled her, his heat continuing to dance over her skin.

Was he checking out her butt? Or deciding if he wanted her for dinner?

Neither possibility was reassuring.

At last completing his circle, the male halted in front of her, meeting her wary gaze with a mysterious smile.

"He had to deal with a personal matter."

Personal matter? What was that supposed to mean?

Tayla narrowed her eyes as her brain was seared with an unwelcome visual of Baine standing in his harem with a bevy of beautiful females kneeling at his feet.

Not that she'd seen any hint of other females when she'd been in his harem. Or even knew what a 'bevy' entailed. But still...

Everyone knew dragons had insatiable sexual appetites.

"Personal?"

His brows arched as he easily read the jealousy she had no right to feel.

"Not that kind of personal," he assured her. "He discovered he has a traitor among his servants."

"Oh." She bit her bottom lip. Baine was taking on a traitor? By himself? "He isn't in danger, is he?"

Char studied her worried expression. "Does the thought trouble you?"

"I..." She wrapped her arms around her waist, belatedly trying to disguise her flare of fear.

It was bad enough to admit to herself she was fascinated by the arrogant Baine. She didn't want it advertised to the rest of the world.

"Only if he leaves me trapped here," she muttered.

Char tilted back his head to laugh with rich amusement. "I thought he'd lost his mind. Now I begin to understand his fascination."

The gray eyes darkened to smoke as Char allowed his gaze to slide down her body, taking a thorough survey of her too-short nightgown.

Tayla heaved a resigned sigh. Was it some sort of dragon rule to flirt with every woman who crossed their path?

"No, you were right the first time," she said dryly. "He's lost his mind."

His smile only widened, his nose flaring as if he was savoring her scent.

"There's something different about you."

Tayla took a step back. "Nope, just a common imp." She shrugged. "Unless you're referring to my baking skills. I have to admit my scones are extraordinary. You should stop by my teashop and try them."

"Hmm." His gaze lingered on her lips. "I wonder what you taste like."

Taste? That couldn't be good. She swallowed a lump that threatened to choke her.

"It's not nice to eat your guests."

He stepped toward her. "Not even a nibble?"

"No."

"I promise you'll like it."

She probably would have. If she'd met him before Baine.

But now...

Almost as if the thought of him had somehow conjured him into being, there was a blast of power that made the ground shake.

"A step closer, Char, and I'll have you skinned and made into a sofa," a deep male voice promised.

They both turned to discover Baine standing in the doorway of the cottage.

Surprisingly nonchalant, considering that Baine's eyes smoldered with an amber fire and his tattoos were swirling over his skin at a dizzying speed, Char glanced toward Tayla.

"There's no need to be selfish," the half-breed protested. "She's a delicate morsel, but there's plenty to go around."

Baine stalked straight toward the male, the air sizzling with a heat that would have fried her if she'd been human.

"When did you develop a death wish?"

Char stood his ground. "About the same time you developed an obsession with imps."

With a blinding speed Baine's arm shot out to wrap his fingers around Char's throat. Then, displaying a terrifying strength, he lifted the half-breed off the ground.

"Mine," he said in soft tones.

Char's face reddened as the fingers bit into his neck, but the half-breed appeared strangely pleased by Baine's violent response.

Was he demented?

"Got it."

"Say it," Baine insisted.

"She's yours, my lord."

"Bull hockey," Tayla abruptly muttered.

The two males exchanged startled glances, as if surprised she was still there. Then an unmistakable hint of amusement tugged on Baine's lips.

"Bull hockey?" he asked, lowering his companion back to the ground.

"I might be temporarily forced to pay for my father's debts, but I don't belong to anyone," she informed him.

"She's going to need some training," Char pointed out, lightly touching the burns on his neck that were rapidly healing.

"True," Baine agreed. "I think I'm up for the task."

Tayla narrowed her gaze, pointing a finger toward the aggravating dragon.

"Your friend isn't the only one with the death wish," she warned.

Char chuckled. "Is she always grumpy when she gets out of bed?"

Heat wrapped around Tayla as Baine moved toward her, a barely leashed hunger tightening his beautiful features.

"I suppose that's something I'll soon discover."

Excitement blistered through her, making her heart pound and her mouth dry.

He was so exotic. And gorgeous. And gloriously male.

Who could blame her heart for leaping with excitement at the mere thought of waking in his arms?

"Baine," she breathed, a flush staining her cheeks.

Char made a choked sound as he studied her blush. "Amazing," he breathed.

Baine nodded in some mysterious agreement. "Yes."

Tayla frowned. What the heck were they talking about? It had to be some dragon thing.

"Did you discover the traitor?" Char thankfully turned the conversation to more important matters.

Baine's face clenched with grim anger. "Fist."

"Damn." Char looked shocked, then his eyes swirled with thunderclouds. "Is he dead?"

"Not yet."

Char's smile made Tayla's blood run cold. "Good. It will be my pleasure to take care of the traitor."

Baine lifted a slender hand. "He's in the dungeon. I want him left alive for now."

Char thinned his lips in frustration. "That sets a bad precedent."

Baine shrugged. "I might need him."

Accepting that his master wasn't going to give him the green light to destroy the traitor, Char gave a grudging nod of his head.

"Fine. What do you want from me?"

"I want you to track down the trolls who broke into Tayla's home," Baine said.

Tayla widened her eyes in surprise. Why was he interested in the trolls?

"That should be simple enough," Char said with a shrug. "What do you want me to do with them?"

"Just keep an eye on them for now."

Char glanced toward Tayla before returning his attention to Baine.

"And you?"

"Go away, Char," Baine muttered as he turned toward Tayla, a strange glitter in his amber eyes.

Tayla was vaguely aware of Char chuckling as he gave a wave of his hand and disappeared into a portal, but it was impossible to concentrate on anything beyond the large dragon who prowled toward her. Especially when he swept her off her feet to cradle her against his chest.

Ignoring her tiny gasp, he carried her into the cottage, a delectable heat cloaking around her.

Lowering his head, he spoke directly in her ear. "Alone at last, my sweet Tayla."

CHAPTER SEVEN

Baine had possessed his share of lovers. He might not be like many dragons who felt the need to indulge their primitive urges with endless orgies, but he was a sexual animal who enjoyed the delights of the female body.

But he couldn't ever remember carrying a woman before Tayla. Why would he? If a female was disabled he would call for a healer.

Now he discovered there was something utterly satisfying in having this particular female in his arms as he entered the small cottage that was a reflection of her deepest desire.

Sucking in a deep breath of her tart scent, he felt her tiny shiver.

She abruptly broke the silence. "Char said there was a traitor."

Baine frowned, studying her flushed face. He'd arrogantly assumed her shiver was one of pleasure.

Had he been mistaken?

Slowly lowering her to her feet in the center of the small living room, he reached to stroke a golden curl that had tumbled over her cheek.

"Are you afraid of me?" he demanded.

"I'm…" Her words faltered, her eyes shimmering with flecks of jade. "I don't know what I am."

His fingers traced the line of her jaw and down the length of her throat.

"Do you want me?"

She licked her lips in an unconscious invitation, inwardly struggling to confess the truth.

"Yes, but I don't want to want you," she at last muttered.

Baine scowled. He'd lived for centuries. Females were always eager to attract his attention. He didn't like the thought she would regret their mutual hunger.

"Because I'm a dragon?"

She blinked, as if baffled by his question. "What do you mean?"

"Are you prejudiced against my species?"

She looked genuinely shocked. "Of course not."

Something eased deep inside him.

"Then why don't you want to want me?"

"Because I was bartered like a piece of property by my own father." She wrinkled her tiny nose. "I'm supposed to be a martyr, not a willing victim."

A martyr? Baine barely suppressed his shudder.

"This has nothing to do with your father."

"Of course it does." She sent him a glare that informed him he was being impossibly dense. "If he hadn't used me to pay his debt to the trolls, you would never have known I even existed."

Baine gave a sharp laugh. Did she know nothing about fate?

Destiny would have eventually crossed his path with this glorious female.

She was his purpose in life.

"Your father's weakness provided the opportunity for our first meeting, but that was not the reason I hunted you for twenty-five years," he said.

A hint of vulnerability softened her features before she was giving a sharp shake of her head.

"Dragons are notorious for protecting their hoard," she muttered. "You couldn't bear the thought that I had escaped."

His fingers moved to touch the thin chain that shimmered in the cresting morning sunlight.

"True." At last they could agree. He would always protect her. "You are mine."

Her eyes widened, her pulse fluttering at the base of her throat. "Stop saying that."

Baine could feel her tension vibrating through her slender body. He didn't understand why she battled against her sensual nature. Or the ruthless power that was drawing them ever closer together.

But he wasn't going to rush her.

Not because he cared about her good opinion, he hurriedly assured himself. He was, after all, a dragon. And dragons were above petty emotions.

But her remark about being a martyr had struck a nerve. He didn't want a female in his bed who was determined to treat their passion as some sort of curse.

He wanted Tayla warm and welcoming and insatiable for his touch.

Which meant he needed to convince her that her place in his harem had nothing to do with her father's debts. And like any good predator, he'd already searched and discovered her weakest points.

In contrast to his previous lovers, Tayla had no interest in gold or jewels. Or even power.

No. She'd spent her life being denied the love and affection that was the foundation of most fey families. She was eager to have someone care for her.

Granted, he didn't have much experience in tending to a female. Actually, he had zero experience.

But how hard could it be?

"I have something for you," he said, grasping her hand to lead her into the kitchen.

"For me?"

Warily she allowed herself to be tugged across the sun-drenched room to the wooden table that was set near the window.

Baine urged her into one of the wooden chairs as he opened the woven basket he'd demanded his servants prepare before returning to the cottage.

With care he set out the platters of home-baked bread with butter and honey still on the comb. There was another platter of fresh fruit and nuts. And last, but not least, was a bottle filled with a golden substance he'd been assured was the very best nectar money could buy.

Opening the bottle, he poured the thick liquid into a glass and settled in the chair across the table to watch in anticipation as Tayla cautiously took a sip.

Her eyes widened in shock. "Where did you get this?"

He watched her lick a golden droplet from her bottom lip, his cock hardening with a painful need.

"Direct from the Chantri," he said, his tone distracted.

She gasped, abruptly setting down the glass. "You have connections with fey royalty?"

He grimaced. He hated dealing with the arrogant Chantri. They had an insane belief that they were equal to dragons. Unacceptable. But they did come in handy on occasion. Like when he needed the finest food to feed his imp.

"I make it a habit to ensure that I have a variety of demons in my debt at all times," he murmured. "I called in a favor owed to me by Prince Magnus."

"Oh." She abruptly set down the glass, studying the bounty spread across the table with a helpless expression.

"Doesn't it please you?"

"Of course."

Baine frowned. She was supposed to be giddy with gratitude. He'd forced himself to waste over an hour traveling to fairyland. Then he'd had to cash in a very useful favor.

Why wasn't she giddy?

"You are..." He hesitated, choosing his words with care. "Very difficult to please."

She reached to grasp a succulent strawberry, studying it as if she'd never seen a piece of fruit before.

"I just don't understand."

"Understand what?"

Lifting her gaze, she studied him in wary confusion. "Why would you trade in a favor for me?"

He shrugged. "It's my duty to make sure you're adequately fed while you're in my care."

"Oh. Duty." Something that might have been disappointment rippled over her pretty features. "I see."

Baine grimaced. He felt oddly embarrassed to admit he'd been determined to please her. No matter what the cost. But then again, he didn't want her to think he would do the same for any other female.

It was all very unnerving.

"And I thought it would make you smile," he grudgingly confessed. "Something that has become important to me."

A charming blush warmed her cheeks. "Baine."

"Eat," he ordered in gruff tones.

"Bossy," she muttered, but she obediently devoured the food with a gusto that filled him with a smug satisfaction. She was more cautious with the nectar, taking small sips as if she wanted to savor each taste. At last she glanced up to discover him watching her with an unwavering fascination. Her blush deepened. "Aren't you hungry?"

Hungry? He was ravenous.

"Not for food," he said in low, husky tones.

She choked on a strawberry, the scent of her arousal spicing the air even as she tried to pretend indifference.

"What do dragons eat?" she asked.

He resisted the urge to lean across the table and lick the strawberry juice from her lips.

Patience...

"I'm a predator," he said. "I eat what I kill."

She wrinkled her nose. "I suppose you hunt in your other form?"

"I do." He paused. Then with a sharp surge he was on his feet and holding out his hand. "Would you like to see?"

She blinked. "See you hunt?"

"See my other form," he corrected, not entirely sure why he was suddenly so determined to witness her reaction to his beast.

He just knew he needed to make sure that she wasn't going to be freaked out by his native form.

"I..." She hesitated, and for a second he feared she might actually refuse. Then, with a hesitant motion, she rose to her feet and placed her hand in his. "Yes. I would like that very much."

An odd relief surged through him as he urged her out the back door.

"Come with me."

He tugged her through the small garden and into the wide meadow that was filled with wild flowers. He left her standing next to a small stream and moved far enough away he wouldn't startle her with his transformation.

Then, keeping his gaze locked on the female who watched him with wide eyes, he released the magic that thundered deep inside him.

With a fiery burst of power he was covered in flames that rolled over his body, transforming his skin to silver scales that expanded as his body elongated. Tayla could hear his bones popping, his muscles and sinew ripping as the beast inside emerged, revealing the lizard-like form with a long, spiked tail and short legs that ended in razor-sharp talons.

His head was heavy, with a narrow snout lined with ten-inch teeth and eyes that glowed with amber fire. And from the center of his back his leather wings spread out in graceful lines.

With his shift completed, Baine shuddered, pure ecstasy seeming to race through him as he shoved off the ground and headed for the sky.

He was…

Tayla struggled for the words that would capture the imposing beauty of the creature soaring above her.

In the cresting sun his scales shimmered like polished silver, the sheen so brilliant it hurt her eyes. In contrast, his wings were as dark as death, slicing through the air with a lethal ease.

She'd always assumed dragons in their native form would be large and bulky, like a flying alligator. But Baine was the complete opposite. He was a sleek, sexy predator who made her shiver in awe.

Watching him circle the sky with a breathless fascination, she didn't even consider scampering backward when he floated down and landed only a few feet away. Heck, she actually stepped forward, indifferent to the claws that dug huge chunks out of the ground and the rush of air that flattened her nightgown against her as he gave a last flap of his massive wings.

Instead she was mesmerized by the amber gaze that was studying her with a fierce intensity, luring her ever closer.

One step forward. And then another. And another. Until she could feel the explosive heat that radiated from the silver body, and a tendril of smoke wrapped around her tense form.

Being this close to Baine was like standing near a volcano that might explode any second. *A very sexy volcano*, a voice whispered in the back of her mind, excitement shivering through her as there was a flurry of magic and the dragon was once again a stunningly handsome male dressed in a pair of loose dojo pants.

"Well?" he demanded, his voice husky and his amber eyes burning with his inner fire.

Still lost in a sense of wonderment, it took Tayla a second to realize he was waiting for her to respond. She blinked, puzzled by his carefully composed expression. Was he seeking compliments? That was...oddly endearing.

"You must know you're magnificent," she said with a shrug. There was no way she was going to admit that she'd been utterly enchanted by the sight of him.

"Yes," he agreed.

Tayla rolled her eyes. "Yeesh."

He stepped toward her, his tattoos swirling over his skin as if he was hiding some intense emotion behind his expression of indifference.

"What I want to know is if my animal form..." He hesitated, clearly choosing his words with care.

"What?" she prompted.

"Bothers you."

She frowned, genuinely baffled by his strange question. "Why would it bother me?"

His gaze remained locked on her upturned face. "The fey tend to be skittish of the larger predators."

She snorted. "Probably because we aren't overly eager to become dinner."

"But you weren't frightened," he pressed.

"No." She'd been far too captivated by his fierce beauty to think of all the reasons she should be terrified. "Obviously I'm either out of my mind or I've reached my fear quota."

He reached out to thread his fingers through her hair, his brooding gaze studying her mouth with an unnerving concentration.

"There's a more logical explanation," he told her.

"And what's that?"

"You want me."

She shuddered at his blunt claim, feeling the urge to purr beneath the stroke of his finger, like a cat.

"Baine," she breathed.

He lowered his head, their noses nearly touching. "Admit it," he commanded.

She planted her hands against his chest. She was going to push him away. At least, that'd been the plan. But as soon as her palms came into contact with the satin heat of his skin she was dangerously distracted.

"Why does it matter?" she muttered, exploring the sculpted muscles that flexed beneath her light touch.

Yow. She'd never realized the male body could be so beautiful.

She could pet him all day.

There was a rumbling sound of pleasure deep in his chest, his fingers tightening in her hair to tilt her head back, exposing her throat.

"When I take you to my bed, I want it to be because you are eager for my touch. Not because it's your duty."

Oh. Tayla struggled to hide her small smile. Clearly her earlier claim that she didn't want to want him had struck a raw nerve.

Now he was determined to prove he could make her forget her pride.

"You're so arrogant," she accused, forgetting how to breathe as his lips blistered a path of kisses down the side of her neck.

"Say the words, Tayla," he insisted, his lips trailing over the dragon marque that rested against the upper curve of her breasts.

Her hands moved to clutch at his shoulders as her knees went weak. Oh lord. His lips were magic. Sheer magic. It was no wonder he had to build a harem to keep the females who were anxious to be his concubines.

Who could blame her if she gave in and...

No. Bad imp.

She dug her nails into his skin, desperately trying to hold on to sanity.

"You can't make me," she stubbornly denied.

Open-mouthed kisses singed over the tender skin of her breasts as his arm lashed around her waist and he pulled her tight against his hard body. Tayla moaned, her nipples acutely sensitive to the heat seeping through the thin fabric of her gown.

"Is that a challenge?" he demanded, lifting his head to regard her with a smug smile. "Accepted."

Tayla swallowed a curse. Yikes. Had she actually just challenged a dragon? Not good. Not good at all.

"No...I..." Her stumbled words were brought to a sharp end as he swooped his head down to kiss her with a stark hunger.

She stiffened, then with a strangled groan, parted her lips.

Desire raced through her like wildfire, her arms instinctively wrapping around his neck as his tongue dipped into her mouth. Yum. He tasted of raw power and exotic spices.

It was addictive.

Tayla lost track of time as he held her tight against his stirring erection, plundering her mouth over and over as she softly moaned.

He was passionate, demanding, and increasingly aroused, but Tayla was acutely aware of the thunderous power he was keeping leashed. It crackled around them like a thunderstorm, filling the air with electricity.

The tingling sensations should have set off all sorts of alarms. She might be stronger than a human, but she couldn't begin to match this dragon in power or magic.

Instead they only intensified her arousal.

Catching her bottom lip between his teeth, he gave it a tiny nip before he lifted his head far enough to study her dazed expression.

"Say the words."

Words? What words? Tayla struggled to think. Oh yeah.

Those words.

She narrowed her gaze. "If I don't?"

He pulled in a deep breath, a wicked smile curving his lips at the heavy scent of her arousal that filled the air.

"Then I'm not trying hard enough to convince you," he warned, abruptly grabbing her around her waist so he could sling her over his shoulder.

"Baine," she shrieked in protest. She didn't have to ask him what he was doing. Not when his long strides were taking them back to the cottage and down the short hallway with dizzying speed. A dangerous anticipation clenched her muscles. "Don't you have some dragon business to take care of?" she muttered.

"Nothing is more important than this," he assured her, bending forward to dump her onto the center of the bed.

She landed with a small bounce, the air knocked from her lungs.

Okay, it wasn't actually landing on the soft mattress that stole her breath. It was the sight of Baine as he leaned over her.

With the morning sunlight threading through the raven darkness of his hair and emphasizing the perfection of his features, she was struck by his otherness. The fey were a beautiful species, and vampires could be drop-dead gorgeous...literally. But Baine's beauty was like a punch to the gut.

So overpowering that it was difficult to believe he was real.

The sense of unreality was abruptly shattered as he reached out and, grabbing the neckline of her nightgown, ripped it in two.

"Hey," she rasped.

With graceful ease, he was kneeling on the mattress next to her rigid body, his eyes burning with an amber fire.

"Don't worry," he said, his hand skimming over her shoulder and down her arm. "I'll buy you a dozen new gowns," he promised, his voice low and hypnotic. "A thousand."

Tayla shivered, acutely aware her nipples were hardening beneath Baine's smoldering survey. Her ego might demand she pretend that sharing a bed with this male was some huge sacrifice, but her body refused to cooperate.

"I can buy my own clothes," she ridiculously muttered.

He gently traced the delicate line of her collarbone. "I want to see you draped in the finest silks."

"That's so…" The words tangled in her throat as his fingers drifted down to tease the sensitive tip of her breast. "Oh."

Planting his hands on each side of her shoulders, he bent downward, replacing his teasing finger with his lips. Oh…yes. The wet heat was exactly what she wanted.

With growing insistence he sucked at her nipple, his glossy hair brushing her face and his hand running a bold trail down the tense muscles of her belly. Everywhere he touched, sparks of acute pleasure shot through her, coalescing in a throbbing ache between her legs.

Tayla hissed, her body bowing as a shimmering, incandescent bliss streaked through her.

His fingers traced the curve of her hip, his head lifting to reveal his expression that was rigid with barely restrained hunger.

"But then again, such amazing skin should never be covered," he husked. "Perhaps I'll keep you in my harem without anything to hide such beauty."

She trembled, not nearly as outraged as she should be by his fantasy of watching her waltz around butt-naked. In fact, she was beginning to appreciate the advantages of allowing his lips and clever fingers free access.

It was only the mention of his damned harem that pissed her off.

"Not even in your dreams," she forced herself to mutter.

His low chuckle brushed over her like a warm caress. Delicious. Almost as delicious as his hand sliding beneath her thigh to tug her legs apart.

Tayla swallowed a moan, her pussy clenching with anticipation. Just the thought of him settling on top of her and filling her with the thick length of his cock was almost enough to make her climax.

What would happen when he actually did it?

Would she combust?

"About those dragon duties," she babbled, suddenly unnerved by the sheer fury of her desire.

It threatened to consume her.

"I'm taking care of the only dragon duty that matters," he told her, his amber eyes holding her gaze as he reached down to yank off his loose pants.

Her nails dug into her palms. *Don't look, don't look, don't look...*

She looked.

And she was lost.

He was just as gorgeous as she anticipated. No. More gorgeous.

No amount of imagining could compare to the sight of his perfectly sculpted body that rippled with lean muscles and shimmered with his hypnotizing tattoos. He looked as if he'd been created by the hand of a master.

And then there was his cock...

Long and hard and thick enough to make her wonder whether or not he would fit.

"Baine," she croaked, too lost in sensations to protest when he moved to settle his hips between her spread legs.

His head lowered, his mouth dropping restless kisses over her heated face before he licked a path down the side of her throat.

"Mmm."

His rumble of pleasure vibrated against her, her hands moving to shove her fingers into the soft thickness of his hair. She'd wondered what it would feel like since she first caught sight of him. Now she knew. Satin. Pure satin.

"I love the taste of you," he muttered, nipping the tender flesh at the base of her neck. "Lemons."

Lemons? Tayla stiffened. That didn't sound very sexy.

"Are you saying I'm sour?" she demanded.

"Tart," he corrected, his lips grazing over her breasts to give each tightly clenched tip a lingering lick. "Tantalizing. Addictive."

Okay. That sounded better. She gave a soft moan as his lips continued to skim downward, the heat of his body blasting through the air. Almost as if he'd opened the door of a furnace to allow his inner fire to sear through the air.

Sensing her startled shiver, he lifted his head to study her with concern.

"Am I too hot?"

A shaky laugh was wrenched from her lips. "If any other male asked me that question I would assume that he—"

Her teasing words were cut off as Baine glared at her with an unexpected anger.

"Don't," he rasped.

Tayla's heart slammed against her ribs. She had a sudden glimpse of the lethal predator that lurked just beneath the surface.

"You won't talk of other males," he commanded, bristling with pure male possession. "You won't even think of them."

Caught off guard by his fierce reaction, she gave a shake of her head.

"What do you mean?"

He leaned down until they were nose to nose. "I'm the only male you will have on your mind." He claimed her lips in a kiss that radiated heat to the tips of her toes. "And in your bed."

CHAPTER EIGHT

Somewhere in Baine's addled brain he knew he was overreacting.

Since when had he considered whether or not a female was thinking about another male? Never. That's when. As long as she was in his arms he just assumed she was there because she was eager to be his lover.

Why wouldn't he? It wasn't like there weren't females lined up to be invited to his harem.

Now, however, he was battling the overwhelming urge to...

To what?

He'd already claimed her with the dragon marque that hung around her neck. Still, there was a restless need deep inside him that demanded more.

Perhaps sensing his avaricious desire to keep her entirely for himself, Tayla eyed him with a wary suspicion.

"Baine..."

"Shh. No more talking." Framing her face in his hands, Baine angled her face upward, kissing with a stark demand.

Mine, a voice whispered in the back of his mind.

Parting her mouth with his tongue, Baine tasted deeply of her tart sweetness, a savage need humming through his body. For a second she remained stiff beneath him, as if still wary of his fierce possessiveness. Then, with a sigh, she arched closer to his body, her fingers sliding through his hair.

"Bossy," she muttered against his lips.

The beast inside him growled in satisfaction, sensing her capitulation.

He brushed his mouth over her eyes, the narrow line of her nose, before returning to her soft lips that seemed to plead for his kiss. At the same time, he was settling deeper between her legs.

They groaned in unison as the head of his cock slid through her moist cleft. Baine clenched his teeth. It would be so easy to slam his way home and put an end to the brutal ache to possess this female. But there was no way he was going to rush through their first time.

Not when he wanted her so lost in her need that she would forget she'd ever been bartered to him by her father.

Nuzzling a tender spot at the base of her throat, he smiled in satisfaction as she tilted back her head to allow him greater access.

Exploring downward, he released a tiny burst of fire that danced over her tender skin. Not hot enough to burn, but sizzling with an erotic heat that made her jerk with startled pleasure.

"That is..." Her words trailed away as he headed downward, taking a puckered nipple between his lips. "So good."

"Perfect," he murmured, savoring her tart taste as he explored over the curve of her breast, and then lower.

Downward, he traveled. Along her narrow ribcage, over the flare of her hips.

She was tiny, but flawlessly curved, and so exquisitely fragile. Like a rare book that needed to be handled with care, he sternly reminded himself.

Leashing the beast inside him, he inched himself down the mattress, sliding his arms beneath her thighs. Then, spreading her legs even wider, he sucked in a deep breath of her enticing arousal.

With a low groan, he tugged her legs over his shoulders, giving him the perfect angle to sweep his tongue through her pussy. His cock twitched as the taste of her filled his mouth.

Damn. It was richer than most imps. A complex mixture, as if she had hidden depths.

At any other time he might have paused to work through the mystery. Dragons loved puzzles, after all. But he was in no mood to halt long enough to question her about the multifaceted flavor that teased at his senses. Not when his tongue was dipping into her tight channel before stroking back to her tender clit.

She quivered, her sharp gasp filling the air. *Ah*. So his little imp liked that. Repeating the caress over and over, he tightened his hold on her legs as she squirmed in delight.

"Enough," she breathed, reaching down to thread her fingers through his hair.

Oh, hell no. It wasn't nearly enough, Baine decided.

If she could still form coherent words, she wasn't as lost in her passions as she needed to be.

"Come for me," he commanded, flicking the tip of his tongue at her precise point of pleasure.

She gave a strangled groan, her fingers tugging on his hair hard enough to cause pain. Not that Baine noticed. He was lost in the delight of watching as her pale face flushed and her eyes darkened until they looked like shimmering emeralds in the sunlight.

Her breath came in small pants, her teeth digging into her lower lip as she finally gave in to the beckoning climax with a sharp cry of bliss. Her entire body shuddered with the force of her orgasm.

Still he continued to stroke her pussy, easing her through her release and immediately reigniting her desire.

"Baine," she groaned, her soft plea luring him back up her body, his lips pausing every inch to plant a teasing kiss against her damp skin.

His fingers cupped her breasts, his thumbs circling the tight peaks of her nipples while his mouth trailed kisses up the curve of her neck.

"Touch me," he demanded, roughly.

With a tiny groan of relief, she instantly complied, almost as if she'd been eager to explore his rigid muscles. Baine muttered a curse, gripping her hips to press her firmly against his aching cock.

He'd intended to savor her for hours. Perhaps days. But the sexy little imp wasn't content with smoothing her hands over his chest. No. She caressed the line of his shoulders and the bulge of his upper arms before slowly following the curve of his spine.

His breath hissed between his teeth as she briefly cupped his ass and then slid her fingers around his hips so she could wrap them around the length of his erection.

At the same time, she lifted her head off the mattress, using the tip of her tongue to trace the tattoos that moved over his skin.

Damn. Bolts of bliss crackled through him, his cock pulsing with an urgent demand for release. There was no way in hell he was going to last another few minutes, let alone the entire day.

Evidently he was going to have to take the edge off his hunger before he considered such an ambitious plan.

Reaching down, he closed his fingers over hers, helping her guide his erection to the entrance to her body. Then, as the broad head rested against her opening, he kept ahold of her fingers, moving them to rub against her clit. Tayla gave a soft moan, her head falling back to the mattress as he stirred the embers of her arousal.

It wasn't until she instinctively wrapped her legs around his hips, widening herself for his penetration, that he at last surged forward, stretching and filling her until he was fully encased in her tight channel.

Gazing down at the woman beneath him, a strange sensation spread through his chest at the sight of the vulnerability that shimmered in her wide eyes. Could she look any more innocent? Like an angel he'd stolen from the heavens. It stirred a protective instinct that sent a chill of alarm down his spine.

No. He violently slammed the door on anything that could distract him from this moment.

Lowering his head he kissed her with a fierce demand, pulling his hips back before surging into her welcoming heat. She groaned in soft encouragement, her hips lifting to meet his powerful thrusts.

Baine slid his tongue between her lips, his dragon rumbling with pleasure as it released a burst of dragon-fire. Unaware they were wrapped in his flames, Tayla returned his kiss with a growing desperation that couldn't be faked.

In this moment she wasn't thinking about her father, or duty, or the payment of a debt—

His thoughts shattered at the raw pleasure that tightened his balls.

He was close. So blissfully close.

Pressing Tayla's fingers tight against her clit, he heard her release a strangled moan, her body clenching around his cock. Unable to hold back any longer, he thrust his hips forward one last time, hissing as his powerful climax exploded through him.

Incandescent flames danced over the bed, twining around their tightly locked bodies as if binding them together.

Damn. What had the female done to him?

CHAPTER NINE

Levet wasn't certain how much the male imp was paying for his lodgings at the pub, but whatever it was, it was too much.

Wrinkling his snout at the stench of stale ale and piss that filled the lower cells, he kept his tail lifted off the sticky floor and pushed open the door that was hidden behind the web of illusion.

If possible, the cramped space was even worse than the outer cells.

There were not only the nasty smells, but there were piles of dirty clothing tossed on the floor along with empty bottles and grimy plates that made Levet shudder in horror.

Clearly Odel was on a downward spiral to hell.

The perfect place for the spineless fool, Levet acknowledged. Unfortunately, he needed the imp to help him rescue Tayla from the dragon. Once Tayla was safe, the imbecile could drown in his rubbish as far as Levet was concerned.

Forcing himself over the threshold, he glanced around the seemingly empty room, relieved that gargoyles were immune to most diseases. Who knew what nasty germs were percolating in the swamp of filth?

Worse, there was no imp lying on the ratty cot or hunkering in a dark corner.

"*Sacrebleu*," Levet muttered, pressing his wings close to his body. "This must be his room, but where is—" His words broke off as he caught the scent of brandy-soaked figs. A minute later a male with long, golden hair and a thin face swayed into the room, wearing a wrinkled white shirt and black slacks. "Odel?" he muttered, watching as the male's yellowish-green eyes narrowed.

"Yes. I'm Odel," the imp said, nearly toppling on his face as he performed an exaggerated bow. "At your service."

Levet gave a click of his tongue. The male was drunk as a skunk. A peculiar saying, considering that Levet had never seen a skunk so much as tipsy.

Then, before he could speak, the imp was giving a frantic shake of his head.

"No. Wait," he mumbled. "I'm not Odel. In fact, I don't even know an Odel. I'm..." His brows furrowed as he ridiculously tried to remember his lies. "What the hell is my name?"

"Odel?" Levet suggested.

"Yes, that's it." Odel grinned, then belatedly realized his mistake. "No." The scowl made a return. "Stop confusing me."

"I am not to blame for your stupidity."

The imp studied him with glazed eyes. "Who are you? Some sort of devil?"

Levet gave a slow shake of his head. "Genetics truly are a baffling thing."

"Gen who?"

Levet stepped forward, yearning to launch a fireball at the drunken fey. Not to kill...just to singe his eyebrows. Unfortunately the place was so soaked in alcohol it would probably explode.

"How could you possibly be related to Tayla?" he instead muttered.

"Tayla?" The male stiffened, grabbing the jamb of the door to keep himself steady. "You know my daughter?"

"I do."

There was a short, painful pause as the blood drained from the male's face.

"How is she?" he at last demanded in a hoarse voice.

Levet snorted. "As if you care."

"Of course I care." Something that might have been regret twisted the male's thin features. "I'm her father."

Levet pointed a clawed finger in his direction. "You have no right to claim that title."

Odel hunched his shoulders, as if Levet had struck him. "You know nothing of me."

"I know that you are a selfish coward who gambled away your soul and when it came time to pay your debts, you sold your daughter to save your own pig," Levet snapped.

"My pig?" The male looked briefly confused. "Oh. You mean bacon?"

"*Oui*. To save your own bacon," Levet said in impatient tones. "It is disgusting."

"I didn't know what else to do," Odel tried to bluster. "They would have killed me."

"And what of Tayla?" Levet demanded.

The male shrugged, his expression that of a petulant child. "They promised she would become a favored consort to a powerful dragon."

Levet shook his head. How could this male possibly be related to generous, sweet, unfailingly kind Tayla?

"At least my mother only tried to murder me," he told the male. "She never pimped me out."

Odel glared at him for a long minute, then with a choked cry he fell to his knees, burying his face in his hands.

"It's true," he blubbered. "I'm a miserable excuse for a father."

"You are," Levet readily agreed. "Parents are meant to protect their children."

Odel glanced up, tears running down his face. "It's too late."

Levet pursed his lips. He might be a bit more sympathetic if he thought the bastard was crying for Tayla and not for himself.

"*Non.* You can still do the right thing," Levet insisted.

"What can I do?"

"Repay the debt and release her."

The imp shook his head, guilt rippling over his face before the petulant expression returned.

"I can't," he muttered. "The money's gone."

Of course it was. Levet rolled his eyes.

"What of your store?" he demanded.

"The trolls have destroyed it."

"Then you have no choice." Levet moved forward, poking the male in the center of the chest. "You will have to offer yourself."

Odel sucked in a horrified breath. It obviously had never entered his mind that he might sacrifice himself to save Tayla.

Puke. No wait—putz. *Stupid putz.*

119

"What good would that do?" he blubbered. "They don't want me."

"Don't be so hasty, imp. For once you might actually have some value," a voice drawled as a male stepped out of a portal that opened directly behind the kneeling Odel.

The stranger had a lean face that had the finely chiseled features of a fey with long black hair, although Levet couldn't detect the usual power that hummed around a demon.

"Shit," Odel breathed, trying to scramble away as the portal stretched even wider, and a full-grown troll stepped into the cramped hallway, his thick head busting through the wooden beams above them. Turning back to Levet, the drunken imp scowled with open disgust. "You set me up."

"Why would I set you up, you ridiculous creature?" Levet protested, waddling toward the first male. He had to be fey. Or at least possess some sort of magical blood. That was the only way he could create portals. Levet halted directly in front of the male, sniffing his leather pants. Hmm...he smelled like celery.*Bleck.* "Are you a fairy?" he demanded.

The creature took a startled step backward, glaring at Levet. "Get away from me."

Levet ignored the male's rudeness. Really, demons should have to take lessons in manners.

"Why are you here?" he demanded.

"The imp is coming with me," the demon said, his gaze locking on Odel, who was crab-walking across his grubby floor.

Was the idiot attempting to escape?

"*Non.*" Levet placed his hands on his hips, puffing out his narrow chest. "I located him first. Finder's keepers. He is coming with me."

The dark-haired male regarded him as if he wondered if Levet was entirely sane, then he waved a slender hand toward the waiting troll.

"Take them both."

Levet let loose a squeal as the behemoth of a troll reached out to grab him by the wings.

Oh...drat.

Tayla struggled to catch her breath as Baine slowly rolled to the side, keeping his arms wrapped tightly around her. In the back of her mind was a niggling voice of warning that threatened to destroy this moment. But even as she tensed, Baine captured her lips in a kiss that blazed through her, searing away her brief attempt at sanity.

Oh yeah, and making her toes curl in wonderment.

Snuggled against him, she tried to think of what to say. She didn't know any pillow talk. And 'thank you for the best sex of my life' seemed a little weird under the circumstances.

So instead she asked the question that'd nagged at her since Baine had brought her to the cottage.

"You didn't tell me why we had to leave your lair," she murmured.

She felt him tense, his lips absently brushing over her damp forehead.

"My father," he said, his voice edged with a sudden anger.

Tayla grimaced. Her brief time in the company of the older dragon had left her with the impression of an aggressive brute who ruled with an iron fist.

Thank the heavens that Baine had purchased her from the terrifying beast.

"What about him?"

121

"He's..." He hesitated, as if debating the proper word. "Unpredictable."

Tayla gave a sharp laugh. She had Odel. It was tough to top him as being the most unpredictable father in the world.

"I know the feeling."

Baine's lips skimmed down the length of her nose before pressing lightly against her mouth.

"Yes, I suppose you do."

She pulled back to study his beautiful face. "The two of you don't get along?"

He shrugged. "Dragons rarely form family bonds. We're solitary creatures by nature, although Synge is always happy to claim me as his son when he wants something from me."

She ignored the strange pang that clutched at her heart at his blunt claim that he was a loner.

"Does he want something now?"

A dangerous heat filled the air. "You."

"Me?" She frowned. Was that a joke? No. Baine might tease, but he never joked. "Why?"

"I don't know, but I intend to find out." There was no mistaking his grim determination despite the fact he was nuzzling a line of kisses along her jaw. "Until then, we'll stay here."

"We?" Surprise and something far more perilous jolted through Tayla at the thought of the two of them spending days, perhaps weeks, alone in the tiny cottage. Somehow she'd assumed he would return to his lair. "You're going to stay here?"

He gave the lobe of her ear a punishing nip. "Where else would I be?"

"I thought—"

"Don't think," he interrupted, capturing her mouth in a kiss that was a deliberate attempt to inflame her senses.

It worked like a charm.

"Baine," she breathed, her heart slamming against her ribs.

"I knew it would be like this," he breathed.

She shivered. "Like what?" she demanded, even as she knew the answer.

Powerful, explosive, overwhelming.

"Perfection," he said, his eyes glowing. "We were clearly destined to be together."

She blocked out his words.

He was right. There was no need to think. Not yet.

In this moment all she wanted to do was feel. And feel. And feel...

Tayla stroked the smooth muscles of his chest, fascinated by the satin heat of his skin. At the same time, she slid her foot up his calf, the movement pressing her closer to the growing thickness of his cock.

Excitement bubbled through her at his ready response. The knowledge that she could stir his primitive desires was as intoxicating as nectar.

"My enchanting imp," Baine growled, crushing her lips with slow, drugging kisses that had her arching in pleasure.

He tasted of dragon-fire. And sex. And power.

A heady combination.

His hands skimmed down her body with an intimate exploration that made her tremble. He caressed the slope of her shoulders, and down the backs of her arms. He molded her breasts, his thumbs teasing her nipples to aching peaks. And all the while he continued to dazzle her with his deep, mind-numbing kisses.

Desire crashed through her, as well as a perilous sensation that she was swift to bury in the back of her mind.

Effortlessly sensing her impatience, Baine rolled her onto her back and covered her with his heavy body, his mouth seeking the sensitive tip of her breast.

He murmured his approval as she scraped her nails down his back, and grasped his hips.

With exquisite skill, he tormented her nipple, his cock rubbing against her clit until she was arching beneath him in a silent plea. He turned his focus to her other breast, his hand sliding beneath her to cup her butt.

"I can't wait," he rasped. "Are you ready?"

Ready? Good lord, she was about to combust.

"Yes," she breathed.

"Tell me you need me," he commanded. "I want to hear the words."

"I need you."

As if her words snapped the leash of his control, Baine gave a low growl and with one hard thrust was buried deep inside her.

Tayla gasped. He was large enough to stretch her to the very limit, but it was an exquisite burn. With a throaty moan she wrapped her legs around his hips and dug her heels into his lower back.

"More," he muttered, burying his face in the curve of her neck.

She trembled as she felt the rough rasp of his tongue against her pulse, an erotic heat dancing over her skin as his body was sheathed in dragon-fire.

Yes. *Yes, yes, yes.*

She dug her nails into his hips, holding on tight as his rhythm quickened. It was so good. Too good.

The combined sensations of heat and his ruthless thrusts were swiftly tossing her into a vortex of bliss. Knowing it was a waste of effort to try and prolong the pleasure, Tayla lifted her hips off the mattress, meeting him thrust for thrust.

She moaned as a burst of dragon-fire surrounded them, binding them together and catapulting them into a mutual orgasm that drenched them both in pleasure.

Lost in a sated haze, she floated in a sense of unreality while Baine nuzzled a path of kisses toward the hollow beneath her ear. At the same time, his hands skimmed up the curve of her waist to cup her swollen breasts.

Baine groaned in satisfaction as her nipples readily puckered in anticipation.

"Mine."

The breath was snatched from her lungs as the awareness of Baine flowed through her with a shocking intimacy. It was like…

She sucked in a shaky breath.

Oh, shit.

Despite the obvious warning signs, it was several hours later before Tayla truly accepted that she was in trouble.

Not just 'crap, my soufflé deflated' kind of trouble. Or 'I forgot to pay the electric bill' trouble.

This was 'oh my god, my entire life has changed' trouble.

She should have known it the second that she'd felt Baine thrust deep into her body. There'd been pleasure. So much pleasure she'd nearly blacked out. But she'd told herself it was the gratification of being in the hands of a talented lover.

Even when she'd felt the unmistakable sensation of their souls merging she'd tried to pretend she didn't realize what was happening.

But now she could no longer deny the blatant truth.

There was a part of her that was convinced this male was her…mate.

As in a forever, and ever, and ever mate.

Thankfully, her stomach growled in protest at the long hours they'd spent without nourishment, and Baine crawled from the bed to collect the last of the bread and honey, as well as the container of nectar, allowing her to consider the dire consequences.

And they were dire.

The fey weren't like many demons. Most of them could choose to be with one partner or a dozen. But when an imp was with a species who mated, like vampires or Weres, it could trigger the latent instinct to be claimed.

Panic fluttered in the pit of her stomach.

What was wrong with her?

Not only had she'd fully participated in her own seduction, but now she was becoming emotionally entangled with the male who'd bartered for her like a piece of property.

Gulping the nectar at a reckless rate, Tayla tried to ignore the dragon who was lying beside her, an indolent smile on his painfully beautiful face.

Yeah, like she could ignore the thunderous heat that pulsed through the air. Or the fact that they were both stark naked.

Still, she needed to try and put some sort of barrier between them. Otherwise he might guess that he'd stirred feelings that should never have been stirred.

How pathetic would that be?

Especially after he'd made a point of telling her that dragons didn't want families, or happily-ever-afters.

Realizing she was becoming maudlin, Tayla turned to set her empty glass on the bedside table.

Watching her with an odd expression of satisfaction, as if pleased that she'd managed to clean her plate, Baine whisked away the tray while holding up the small container of nectar.

"One more shot?" he asked.

"No." She shook her head. Any more and she'd be singing sailor ditties and wearing a lampshade on her head. "It's very potent."

He chuckled. "It must be. It's turned your nose red."

She lifted a hand to touch her nose that had gone numb. "It is not."

Baine leaned forward to kiss the tip. "It is still quite charming," he assured her, his words a throaty purr. "Along with your lips." He brushed his mouth over her tingling lips before moving to trace the shell of her ear. "And ears and—"

Erotic pulses of pleasure blazed through her with each destructive caress. Instinctively, she tilted her head to the side, silently inviting him to trail his mouth down the curve of her neck.

It was only when she felt her blood heating in anticipation of his touch that she realized what she was doing. *Yeesh.* She was supposed to be building barriers, not melting beneath the exploring lips.

Forcing herself to lean away from his intoxicating expertise, she tugged the sheet up to her neck.

"What time is it?" she demanded.

Baine arched a brow, easily reading her discomfort. "Time has no meaning in this place."

That was true enough. A few hours might have passed since they entered the cottage, or a month.

"Maybe not, but we can't stay here forever."

The amber eyes studied her with an unnerving intensity. "Why not?"

"Because…"

"Yes?"

She struggled to think of an excuse that might give her an hour or so of breathing room.

"I need to check on my house," she finally managed to mutter.

"It's not going anywhere."

"Maybe not, but I have repairs that need to be made and the entire place needs to be cleaned," she babbled.

He looked less than impressed by her hasty excuse. "The gargoyle can take care of it."

"It's not Levet's responsibility," she insisted. "It's mine."

There was a long, uncomfortable silence before he reached out to gently tuck a stray curl behind her ear.

"What's wrong?"

She shivered. What would he do if she told him?

Oh hey, Baine, I know I'm just a temporary concubine who is here to work off thousands of dollars for my father, but I think you ignited my mating instincts...

He would either laugh or use her weakness to his advantage.

Neither was acceptable.

She grimly held on to her excuse. "My house was destroyed by trolls."

"This has nothing to do with your house."

"Are you a mind reader?"

"Tayla." He framed her face in his hands, studying her with a rising impatience. "Talk to me."

She hunched her shoulders, wishing his exotic scent wasn't saturating the air. It was bad enough that he was gorgeous and naked, with hypnotizing tattoos. Did he also have to smell yummy?

"There's nothing to say."

His eyes narrowed. "Just a few minutes ago you were—"

She hastily pressed her hand to his mouth. She knew what she was doing a few minutes ago.

And it involved her lips being wrapped around his very hard cock...

"Don't," she rasped.

"And now you're anxious to get away from me," he continued, the air prickling with a heat more angry than sexy. "Why?"

She licked her lips, glancing over his shoulder at the window. Anything to avoid that burning amber gaze.

"I might be forced to be your concubine, but that doesn't mean I can pretend my real life doesn't exist," she insisted.

She didn't consider the words tumbling out of her mouth. Not until she felt Baine stiffen.

"Forced?" he said, his voice a low growl.

Tayla grimaced. *Rats.* She'd wanted to put some distance between them, but she hadn't intended to imply that she'd been some sort of unwilling victim.

With an effort, she met his fierce glare. "You know what I mean."

"As a matter of fact, I don't. It sounded as if you were saying that I forced you into my arms." His face was dangerously devoid of emotion. "Am I mistaken?"

"I just meant..." She licked her lips, her gaze once again moving to the window. "I have a life that I can't put on hold forever."

His hands tightened on her face. "Tayla, look at me."

It was a command, not a request, and Tayla found herself obeying before she could stop herself.

"What?"

He bent his head until they were only an inch apart, a small tendril of smoke curling from his nose.

"Are you in this bed because you wanted me or because you felt compelled to be here?"

"Baine—"

"Answer the question," he snarled. "Why are you in my bed?"

They both knew why. She couldn't resist him.

Heck, she didn't *want* to resist him. At least her body didn't.

But the words refused to leave her lips. Instead she gave a shake of her head.

"Do you have to take everything?"

He scowled at her harsh accusation. "What the hell does that mean?"

"Isn't it enough that I've agreed to pay my father's debt?"

"No, it isn't." The amber eyes darkened. Not with anger. But with something that made her heart clench with regret.

Her lips parted to take back the awful words, but before she could speak he was off the bed and yanking on his loose pants.

"Fine." The indulgent lover was gone. Replaced by a cold-eyed predator who snapped his fingers with impatience. "Get dressed."

Acutely aware that she'd just destroyed something fragile, and perhaps even precious, Tayla scrambled off the bed, keeping the sheet wrapped around her shivering body.

"Where are we going?" she demanded.

The perfect male features were hard, the tattoos swirling over his body at a frenetic pace.

"If you want to be treated like another pretty bauble in my hoard, then your wish is my command."

CHAPTER TEN

Baine couldn't remember when he'd been so furious.

Not when his father had tossed him out of the family lair before he'd barely passed puberty. Not when the goblin tried to sell him a treasure chest full of fool's gold. Not even when a mob of overly-zealous humans snuck into his cave and tried to stab him with a pitchfork.

And it *was* fury that flowed through his veins like acid, he grimly assured himself. It had nothing to do with disappointment, or thwarted desire, or an aching heart.

That would be...madness.

Holding onto Tayla's arm, he opened a portal directly to the deepest, most secret part of his lair. Then, tugging her forward, he slammed shut the opening behind them.

Once he sensed she was steady on her feet, he released his grip and took a sharp step backward, folding his arms over his chest.

He told himself it was to be even more intimidating. As if a big, bad dragon needed extra effort to bully a tiny slip of an imp. But that was better than admitting it was the only way to keep himself from reaching out to brush back the golden curls that framed her pale face. Or to touch the plum cashmere sweater to see if it was as soft as it looked.

Inside him his beast lashed its tail and breathed fire. It didn't understand why he wasn't back in bed with this female in his arms.

The beast didn't care that she was stubbornly refusing to admit she melted beneath his touch because she desired him. Desperately. The dragon only knew that nothing had ever felt so good as the sensation of having his cock plunged deep into the silken warmth of her body.

Baine, however, was deeply offended at being accused of forcing a female.

Hadn't he paid a damned fortune for her? And hadn't he spent twenty-five years trying to track her down? And hadn't he taken her to her own slice of paradise so she would be happy to spend her time with him? Hell, he'd traded away a favor from a fey royal so she could have the finest nectar.

And for what?

If her pride demanded she be treated like a prisoner, then fine.

He'd treat her like prisoner.

He pretended he didn't notice her vulnerable expression as she glanced around the massive space that was stuffed to the ceiling with piles of gold and jewels and unusual pieces of art that had captured his attention over the years. His precious books were in a temperature-controlled library that was hidden behind layers of illusion at the far end of the room.

At last she sent him a wary frown. "Where are we?"

"My treasure vault," he drawled, his voice cold. "Make yourself comfortable."

She flinched, wrapping her arms around her waist. "You don't intend to leave me here, do you?"

"Why not?" he growled. "I tried to offer you a pleasant home, but you preferred to be treated as my property." He nodded toward a stack of gold bars. "This is where I keep my spoils of war."

"Baine—"

"I'll return when I have need of you," he rudely interrupted, heading toward the nearby entrance.

"No." Tayla hurried behind him. "Please wait."

Ignoring her plea, he walked out and slammed the door behind him. Dammit, he wasn't going to feel guilty.

Or lonely.

Or...

"My lord."

With a blink, Baine realized the guard who stood on perpetual duty in front of the door to his treasure room was regarding him with blatant concern.

Deliberately he studied the young male who was a half-breed like Char, although he had short black hair and eyes that were a brilliant blue.

"Torque."

"Yes, my lord?"

Make sure no one is allowed near the door," he commanded. "I don't care who they are. Only I'm allowed inside."

The younger male blinked in confusion. It was the same order every guard received when they were given the duty of protecting his hoard. There was no actual need for Baine to repeat himself.

"Of course," he murmured.

"And alert me at once if my father makes an unexpected appearance," he continued.

The guard nodded. "Aye, sir."

Baine still hesitated, feeling oddly uneasy at leaving Tayla.

It wasn't exactly fear. After all, there was no one who could possibly enter his treasure room. Not only was it constantly guarded, but it was wrapped in spells that made sure only he could form portals inside it.

No. It was more a feeling of...unease.

As if he turned his back on the beautiful imp she might slip away.

With a shake of his head at his ridiculous imaginings, Baine forced himself to walk to his private rooms. There was no way in hell that Tayla was escaping.

"Char," he called out, using his mental ties with his loyal servant to open a portal.

Seconds later the half-dragon stepped into the room that was filled with bookcases and deeply cushioned chairs. With his short silver hair brushed from his lean face, and wearing a black turtleneck sweater and black slacks, he looked like an overly pampered tourist who traveled the world in search of excitement. As long as one didn't get too close to the heat that pumped from his sleekly muscled body or caught sight of the storm clouds that swirled through his eyes.

"This is a surprise," the younger male drawled, studying Baine with a raised brow.

Baine moved to pour himself a large glass of his finest brandy.

"What is?"

"I didn't expect to see you out of bed for a month," Char happily explained. "Why aren't you with your lovely imp?"

A good question.

"She is…"

"Beautiful?" Char suggested. "Sexy? Irresistible?"

All three, he silently acknowledged.

Out loud he said, "Aggravating."

Char shrugged. "She's a woman. She's supposed to be aggravating."

Baine swallowed the brandy in one gulp, lifting his hand to rub the back of his neck. Damn. Even with her locked away he felt as if she was glaring at him from the shadows.

"She is doing an excellent job," he muttered, narrowing his gaze as Char gave a sharp laugh. "What's so amusing?"

"I have never seen you so twisted over a female."

Smoke curled from his flared nose. "Twisted?"

Char gave a lift of his hands. "What would you call it?"

"A pain in the ass," he growled, still rubbing his neck. What the hell? The female imp had clearly rattled his mind. "Did you locate the trolls?"

Char hesitated, as if considering continuing the very dangerous game of teasing his master. Then, easily sensing that Baine was at the edge of his patience, he allowed his smile to fade.

"I did," he said in brisk tones. "I followed the trail from your female's lair to a spot just a mile away."

Tiny flames flickered over Baine's skin. Just the thought of the trolls lurking near Tayla's home was enough to make the beast inside him roar with the lust to burn them to ashes.

"They're keeping watch on the house," he said, his expression grim. "That was only to be expected."

Char gave a slow nod. "Yes."

Baine set aside his empty glass. "There's more?"

"I found a portal near the edge of their camp."

A portal? Baine hissed in shock. "Imp?"

"Fairy."

Well that was…unexpected. What the hell would a fairy be doing with a troll? The two species hated each other. Just one more baffling question on a very long list.

"Did you follow it?" he demanded.

"I did."

Baine made a rough sound of impatience. Since when did getting information from Char become worse than pulling fucking teeth? And why did his neck continue to prickle like he was being watched?

His sour mood became downright pissy.

"And?" he snapped.

"It led to an abandoned castle on the border of Norway," the younger male revealed.

Baine held out his hand, waiting for the rolled up map to appear. Then, moving to the desk, he spread it across the flat surface.

"Show me," he ordered.

Char was swiftly at his side, pointing toward an isolated spot.

"Here."

Baine studied the rough terrain. Not the sort of place that would attract most fey.

"A troll stronghold?"

"No." Char gave an emphatic shake of his head. "I couldn't do a thorough sweep of the area, but I suspect they're assassins."

Baine tapped a slender finger on the desk. From what he knew of the ruthless mercenaries, they charged a fortune. Unless they were desperate, few demons were willing to pay the price.

"Since when have the trolls started to hire assassins?"

"I don't have a clue." Char shrugged. "But it has to have something to do with your imp."

Baine felt his heart skip a beat. And not in a good way.

It was bad enough that the trolls and his father were weirdly interested in Tayla. The last thing he needed was a group of assassins joining the madness.

"Why do you say that?"

"Less than an hour ago, a mongrel fairy along with Skragg made an appearance at the castle."

Baine narrowed his gaze. Skragg was the troll who'd originally offered Tayla to his father.

"Could you hear what they were saying?"

"No, but I did catch sight of their prisoners."

"Prisoners? Who were they?"

"A male imp who goes by the name Odel, and a miniature gargoyle."

Baine released a frustrated hiss. He should have known Odel would be up to his neck in trouble. The idiot was born to be an anchor around Baine's neck.

"Why would—" Baine bit off his words as there was a wrenching sense of loss that nearly sent him to his knees. "Shit," he breathed, pressing a hand to the center of his chest.

It took a second to realize what the aching emptiness meant. No surprise. Never in his very long life had he been so connected to a female that he could actually feel her deep inside him.

Only Tayla had ever accomplished that alarming feat.

Flames danced over his skin as Baine stalked out of his private rooms and down the hallway. Swiftly, Char was next to him, his eyes darting from side to side as if searching for an enemy to slay.

"What the hell is going on?" the younger male demanded.

"She's gone," Baine snarled, his pace never slowing as they headed directly for his treasure room.

Char frowned in confusion. "Tayla?"

Something that might have been pain sliced through Baine's chest.

"Yes."

"That's impossible."

"Unless someone assisted her departure," he pointed out, halting in front of the guard. "Torque," he barked.

The male flinched, ogling Baine's flames that had intensified to a pure white heat. Hot enough to singe a half-breed.

"Yes, my lord?"

Baine stepped forward. "Did I not make my orders clear?"

The male gave a jerky nod. "Crystal clear."

"Then why did you open the door?"

Torque paled. "I didn't."

Baine scowled. The young soldier wasn't an idiot. He would have to know that lying to his master was a certain death sentence.

"Someone must have entered the treasure room," he snapped, assuming there must be yet another traitor.

"No, my lord. No one has come in or out," the young man insisted. "I swear."

Muttering a curse, Baine stepped past the sweating guard and shoved open the door.

Together with Char he entered the room and made a quick search among the piles of treasures. Not that it was necessary. The emptiness that continued to throb in the center of his being was enough to tell him Tayla was gone.

"You left her in here?" Char asked, as if Baine had somehow forgotten where he'd stashed the beautiful imp.

"Yes."

"Where did she go?"

"That's the question, isn't it?" Baine snapped, the beast inside him desperate to get out and hunt down the female who he considered his own. Pacing around a large chest filled with precious rubies, he came to an abrupt halt. "Here," he muttered, bending down to touch the floor. He could feel the magic that lingered from a powerful spell. "A portal."

Char made a strangled sound of disbelief. "No demon can create a portal into the treasure room of a dragon."

"Clearly one did," Baine muttered, even as he silently agreed with his companion.

There was no way any creature should have been capable of creating an opening into his lair. Let alone into this heavily spelled area. It was simply inconceivable.

Sifting through the threads of magic, he released a startled breath. The portal had been made by an imp.

"Tayla." With an abrupt movement Baine was straightening, his brows snapping together. None of it made sense. Not unless... "Shit." Baine shook his head, wondering how the hell he could have been so blind. "That's it."

Char moved to stand at his side. "What's it?"

"I've been an idiot." Baine slashed his hand through the air, ripping open a portal that would allow him to follow his aggravating female. "Let's go."

Tayla wondered what'd happened to her.

139

For years and years, she'd been a sober, hardworking business owner who kept a low profile and avoided any risk.

Now she was clearly suicidal.

What else would explain her refusal to wait in Baine's treasure room as she'd been commanded?

She had, after all, promised to pay her father's debt. In fact, she'd rubbed in her acceptance of her duty to the point that she'd actually managed to hurt Baine's pride. A knowledge that oddly filled her with an aching regret.

But while she might have asked for his angry reaction, she'd refused to remain in his hoard simply waiting for him to seek her out when he decided he wanted her back in his bed. They needed to talk. She needed to explain that…

Well, she wasn't sure what she was going to say, but she wasn't going to wait around to say it.

So, she'd opened a portal to follow him, only to overhear his conversation with Char.

She'd briefly forgotten her tangled emotions, her annoyance with Baine, and even her fear at being discovered by the trolls. Levet and her father were in danger.

She had to do something to save them.

Memorizing the spot Char had pointed to on the map, she'd formed a portal to the mountainous castle. No surprise that it'd been an ugly gray monstrosity that served as an impenetrable fortress. Her luck wasn't good enough for her destination to be an elegant spa where she could have a nice facial and massage after she'd managed to rescue Odel.

Creeping as close to the sixteen-foot stone walls as she dared, she'd created another portal that opened into the lowest level of the inner tower.

Then, terrified she was going to be caught at any second, she'd crept through the dark dungeons until she at last caught the unmistakable scent of granite.

Levet.

Glancing around to make sure there were no guards nearby, she found a piece of wire that'd been dropped on the ground and quickly picked the heavy lock. Her father hadn't taught her much over the years, but he had insisted she know how to spot counterfeit money, how to cry on cue, and how to pick a lock.

None of it had been of any use.

Until this moment.

As quietly as possible, she pushed the heavy door open, her choking fear easing as the tiny demon jumped off the narrow cot and waddled toward her.

"*Mon dieu,*" Levet breathed, his wings quivering with shock. "How did you get in here?"

Tayla frowned. Had the poor thing been dropped on his head? How did he think an imp had managed to enter a heavily guarded troll stronghold?

"I made a portal." She spoke slowly. Just in case his brain was addled.

Levet blinked. "Here?"

Yep. It had to be a blow to the head.

"Why not?"

"There is a layer of dampening magic wrapped around the castle," the gargoyle pointed out, staring at her as if he was trying to figure out a puzzle. "I have been unable to produce so much as a fireball."

Tayla shrugged. "As I have said, I have a talent for creating portals. My father said that I inherited the gift from my mother."

Abruptly distracted, the tiny demon wrinkled his snout. "Ah *oui,* your father."

Tayla swallowed a sigh. She was accustomed to that tone of aversion whenever anyone spoke of Odel.

"How did you meet?"

Levet gave a lift of his hands. "I went in search of him."

"Why?"

"It was the only way I could think to save you from the dragon."

"Oh." Tayla's throat tightened as tears filled her eyes. For as long as she could remember, she'd been expected to be the adult. She protected her father from the endless collectors who showed up on their doorstep, and ensured he made it to his bed when he'd indulged in too much nectar. No one had ever thought that she might need to be rescued. "That's so sweet."

"*Sacrebleu.*" Levet rubbed his stunted horn, his tail twitching around his feet. "You are not going to cry, are you?"

She sniffed, battling back the tears. "It's just...no one has ever wanted to save me before."

Reaching out, Levet gently patted her hand. "I did not do a very bang-bang job, did I?"

Tayla's lips twitched. Only Levet could make her laugh in the middle of a dark, dank dungeon that reeked of troll.

"Bang-up?" she corrected.

"*Oui.*" Levet heaved a small sigh. "I had intended to bring Odel to the dragon in exchange for you, but I barely had time to locate him in a London pub when a strange fairy appeared along with a troll."

Tayla gave her friend a pat on the head in gratitude before turning her thoughts to her father's latest disaster.

It was rare for a fey to be working with a troll. The two species hated each other.

"Did they say why they wanted my father?" she inquired.

Levet muttered something that sounded like a French cuss word.

"*Non*, but it is not difficult to guess."

Tayla wrinkled her nose. There was only one reason anyone would actually go out of their way to find her father.

"He owes them money, doesn't he?" she demanded with a sigh.

Levet's wings fluttered, his hands pressing against her legs. Almost as if he was trying to herd her toward the open cell door.

"No doubt he does, but that is not the reason they brought him to this isolated castle."

She allowed herself to be pushed out of the cell. "Then why?"

"It is a trap, *ma belle*. That is the only reasonable explanation." The ugly little face was tense with an increasing concern. "You have to get out of here."

He was right.

It was too great a coincidence to have trolls hunting her and then for her father to be snatched by one. It had to be connected.

Still, she'd come to the castle with a purpose.

"Not without you," she muttered, reaching down to grab Levet's arm. "Or my father."

"Tayla." Levet scurried to keep up, his tail sticking straight out behind him. "Wait."

She shook her head, turning down a narrow tunnel as she sniffed the air for her father's scent.

"We need to hurry," she muttered.

Levet tugged at her hand. "Stop."

She grudgingly came to a halt to study her companion with blatant impatience.

The tunnel was grimy, dark, and the walls were slick with mold. Not to mention the fact that her presence was going to be noticed any second.

Now didn't seem a good time to stand around and chat.

"Why?"

Levet's wings drooped. "Your father."

Tayla sucked in a sharp breath. "He isn't hurt, is he?"

"Non." The wings drooped even lower. "He is the sort who always manages to walk away from a disaster unscathed."

"I suppose he does," Tayla agreed. Odel made sure he survived. No matter what the cost. "So what's wrong?"

Levet hesitated before heaving a noisy sigh. "I do not believe your father is worth risking your life."

"Oh." Tayla bit her lip. She knew Levet was genuinely concerned for her. Which was really quite wonderful. But she'd spent her entire life taking care of Odel. She couldn't just walk away when she knew he was in trouble. "He's my father."

"Such a pity," Levet muttered.

Tayla grimaced, once again pulling Levet down the tunnel. There was no way for her to explain why she felt the need to protect her father.

Probably because there was no excuse for family.

They just…were.

Desperate to find her father and get the heck out of the nasty dungeons, Tayla rounded a corner, only to discover the path was blocked by a seven-foot male with a square face and blond hair buzzed close to his skull.

Wearing a T-shirt and jeans, he might have been a human, but Tayla could smell the troll blood that ran through his veins. As if the hint of crimson in his eyes didn't give away his mixed heritage.

"Ah. At last." The male smiled, revealing his razor-sharp teeth. "I've been waiting for you a very long time, my dear."

CHAPTER ELEVEN

Baine crouched behind the large boulder on top of the mountain and gazed down at the castle directly below him.

When he'd followed Tayla's portal, he'd expected to end up in her house. She'd been annoyingly anxious to return to the cramped building to see to the necessary repairs. Wasn't that why she said she needed to leave his arms?

Instead they were perched in…Baine tilted back his head and sniffed the air.

Norway?

Shit.

"This is the assassins' lair?" he growled.

Char crouched beside him, peering down at the recently repaired ruins.

"Yes."

Baine scowled. There was only one reason she could have come to this place. To rescue that ridiculous gargoyle. Or her even more ridiculous father.

But how could she have known...

Abruptly Baine recalled the odd prickles on his neck. He'd dismissed them way too easily.

Now he realized the tricky imp must have created a portal to spy on him. Then when she'd overheard Char revealing that her father and the gargoyle had been captured, she'd come here to...

Well, he wasn't sure. But he would bet his entire hoard that it included risking her beautiful neck.

"Damn," he muttered as smoke curled from his nostril, flames dancing around his feet.

Suddenly the crisp air was steamy hot.

Char turned so he could study Baine with an unwavering gaze. "Are you going to tell me what the hell is going on?"

His hands grasped the boulder, his thoughts becoming increasingly distracted as his primitive beast desperately tried to catch the scent of his female.

Where was she? Had she already entered the castle?

"Twenty-five years ago, I bartered my father for Tayla."

Char arched a brow. "Yeah, I remember. You've been in a pissy mood ever since then."

Baine ignored the insult.

"I returned to my lair to collect the payment as well as to prepare the harem," he explained in distracted tones.

"Prepare the harem?" Char predictably probed. "What does that mean?"

Baine scowled, his attention never leaving the castle. "None of your damned business," he snapped, not about to reveal that he'd had the entire harem cleaned to make sure there were no traces of other women.

Char made a sound that could have been a choked laugh. "Okay."

Baine ignored the younger male's amusement, too busy counting the various guards he could detect walking the ramparts.

"When I came back, my father didn't bother to tell me the female had disappeared," he continued, turning his attention to the layers of magic that shimmered like a dome over the crumbling inner courtyard. "Not until I'd handed over the payment."

"Typical of Synge," Char growled.

"Exactly." At the time he'd been furious. And not because his father had screwed him out of a fortune. He couldn't believe the fascinating female had slipped from his grasp. And it was that anger that'd blinded him to the obvious. "I assumed she managed to escape through the portal the trolls used to return to this world. But now..."

He allowed his words to trail away, his entire body quivering as he caught the distant scent of burnt lemons.

Tayla.

And she wasn't happy.

"You think she created a portal of her own," Char breathed in astonishment.

Baine shrugged. Under normal circumstances, he would be as stunned as Char by Tayla's outrageous skill. But these weren't normal circumstances.

Not when he was consumed by his frenzied need to get her out of the castle and back to his lair.

"She must have," he said with a shrug.

"Amazing," Char breathed.

"Not amazing." He at last turned his head to glare at his companion. "Dangerous."

Char gave a lift of his brows. "Why dangerous?"

"Clearly my father realized that Tayla possessed the ability to slip in and out of his lair unnoticed." Baine shuddered. Just saying the words was enough to make his gut clench with dread.

Char grimaced. "Oh."

"Exactly." Baine nodded toward the castle below them. "And since Skragg has been hunting her, I assume he must have suspected her talent as well."

"That would explain the overwhelming interest in a mere imp," Char murmured.

"Yes. The trolls want to use her to sneak into a dragon's hoard." The boulder abruptly shattered beneath the force of Baine's tight grip. "And my father wants her dead."

"Damn." Char looked genuinely outraged. No surprise he'd already fallen beneath Tayla's sweet charm. "What's the plan?"

Baine shook his head, struggling to think clearly.

"I go in and get her," he said, his voice thickening with the power of his dragon.

"That's it?" Char reached to grab his arm. "That's the plan?"

Baine tried to shake off the male's restraining grasp. "You want more? How about I kill anyone who gets in my way?"

Char held on tight. "Baine, that's a terrible plan," he muttered.

A low, warning growl rumbled in Baine's chest, the stone melting beneath his feet.

"She's mine."

"Yeah, I got that," Char hastily agreed. "She's yours. But if you go charging in there they might kill her before we can get her back."

Baine hissed, nearly combusting at the mere mention of Tayla being harmed.

He would raze the earth if they harmed her.

With an effort, he forced himself to concentrate on his companion.

"Do you have a better idea?"

"Yeah." Char pointed toward the sky that was painted with the brilliant colors of dusk. "You distract them and I'll sneak in and rescue her."

The earth trembled beneath their feet. It was his female who needed rescuing.

He wanted to be the hero.

"Why don't I rescue her?" he snapped.

Char glanced toward the large crevice that had split open just behind them, smiling with wry amusement.

"Because you're a bigger distraction."

Okay. He couldn't argue with Char's logic. There were few things more distracting than a full-grown dragon preparing to cause utter destruction.

He reached out to lay a hand on his friend's shoulder. "I'm depending on you, Char."

"I'll get her," the younger man said in somber tones. "I swear."

With no choice but to depend on his servant, Baine rose to his feet and jumped off the edge of the mountain. The wind rushed past him as he spread his arms, and with one burst of magic he released the beast inside him.

Tayla swallowed a scream as she took a hasty step backward. There was an unnerving emptiness in the male's crimson eyes that sent a chill racing through her.

This was not a nice man.

And whatever reason he'd lured her to this castle couldn't be a good one.

In fact, she was sure it was very, very bad.

"Who are you?" she rasped, instinctively shoving Levet behind her.

He stepped forward, towering over her in the cramped tunnel.

"Craven."

She tilted her chin, pretending she wasn't afraid. A wasted effort, of course. The male had enough demon blood to smell the terror that pounded through her.

Still, she had her pride.

"Should I recognize the name?"

"Good god, I hope not," he drawled, sounding remarkably polished considering his heritage.

She'd bet her favorite scone recipe that he hadn't been educated by his troll relatives. The nasty demons tended to communicate with grunts, growls, and head-butts.

"I devote a considerable effort to remaining in the shadows," he continued, his gaze sweeping down her tense body. "We do, however, have a mutual friend."

"Who is that?" she demanded.

"Skragg."

Tayla hissed in disgust. She would never, ever forget the revolting creature. He'd not only kidnapped her and sold her to Baine's father, but he'd clearly taken enjoyment in her distress.

"That vile troll isn't my friend."

"Now that's a little harsh, my dear," Craven mocked. "You made quite an impression on him."

"I can't imagine why." She felt Levet pinch the back of her leg. Was he offering a painful warning not to say anything stupid? Or was he trying to pass along some hidden message? "I'm just one of thousands of slaves he's traded."

Craven shook his head, his smile widening. *Yikes.*

"No, you're not just one of the crowd, my dear," he assured her. "You have very unique talents."

"You want me to bake you a teacake?" She winced as Levet gave her another pinch.

Dang it. She was going to be black and blue.

"Perhaps later." The male studied her with an unnerving intensity. "First you're going to open a portal for me."

Oh. Tayla frowned. That didn't seem so bad.

Certainly better than being roasted over a hot fire.

Or raped.

"That's it?" she demanded, certain there had to be a catch.

"It's a very special portal." Craven's chuckle made Tayla shudder. It sounded…evil. "Or should I say, it goes to a very special place."

"Where?" she forced herself to ask.

"A dragon hoard," he answered in smooth tones.

Yep. There was the catch.

She didn't need Levet's pinches to warn her that she had to be careful. Really, really careful.

"That's impossible," she said.

"So I assumed." The crimson eyes narrowed. "Until Skragg was telling a tavern full of drunken demons about a pretty young imp who'd managed to escape from the mighty Synge's lair."

Damn that Skragg. Someday she hoped that he was…well, she wasn't sure what would be an appropriate punishment, but it needed to be painful.

And slow.

"It was an accident," she attempted to bluff. "When the trolls were leaving—"

"No," Craven sharply interrupted. "Skragg was in the lair when it was discovered you'd escaped. Synge was very vocal in his outrage that you'd manage to create a portal."

She licked her dry lips. "He was mistaken."

Without warning the male's hand shot forward, his fingers wrapping around her throat.

"Don't lie to me, imp," he hissed, his eyes glowing crimson in the gloom.

"Leave her alone, you bully." Levet charged around Tayla, his claws curled as he futilely tried to cast a spell. At the same time, Craven lifted his foot to kick the poor creature down the tunnel. "Eek," the gargoyle screeched, hitting the wall with a loud thud.

Or maybe it was something else making the thud, she distantly realized as the tunnel shook and dirt fell from the ceiling.

It was difficult to think when her throat was being crushed.

"No more games," Craven snarled, yanking her off her feet. "You'll open a portal or I'll kill your father."

"Please," she rasped, knowing she was mere seconds from passing out.

How was she supposed to open a portal if she was unconscious?

And what the heck was that thudding? It kept getting louder. As if the castle above them was being methodically destroyed.

"Now what?" she heard Craven mutter before there was the nasty stench of troll filling the air and Tayla was abruptly released. Dropped to the ground, she sucked in painful gasps as the male turned toward the lumbering demon who was far too large for the tunnel. "Skragg? What the hell is going on up there?"

The troll hunched over, his tusks covered with spittle as he struggled to speak.

"Dragon," he at last managed to get the word out.

Craven jerked, his expression one of stark horror. "Fuck."

The troll looked equally alarmed. "F-fire," he stammered.

Shoving herself to a kneeling position, Tayla felt her heart leaping with hope.

It was Baine.

Now that she wasn't being choked to death, she could actually sense him. Not as one demon sensing another. But as a female recognizing her mate.

With a grimace, Craven shoved his way past the lurking troll.

"Keep guard. I don't want them left alone for a second," he commanded. "Got it?"

The troll made a garbled sound, his large form blocking the tunnel as Craven disappeared into the darkness.

Tayla remained on the ground, trying to clear her foggy brain.

They had to escape. Not only because she wasn't going to be used as some sort of dragon thief for Craven and the trolls. But also because she didn't know how much longer the tunnel was going to last.

Larger clumps of dirt and stone were falling from the ceiling as the thudding continued.

What was Baine doing up there?

Once her brain cleared she could create a portal, but she still didn't know where her father was being held. So how did she locate Odel when there was a very large troll blocking her path?

There was the faint sound of claws scratching against the stone floor as Levet limped to stand beside her.

"I believe they made your dragon angry, *ma belle*," he murmured softly.

"He isn't my dragon," she instinctively protested, even as a warm glow flared through her heart.

"Try telling him that," a male voice drawled.

Caught off guard, Tayla lifted her head, watching in shock as Skragg's head tumbled off his body and bounced down the tunnel.

Okay. She'd hoped that the troll would suffer, but yeesh...

Placing her arms around Levet, she scooted away from the disgusting face that was frozen in shock, barely noticing when Skragg's body was tossed aside.

Instead her attention was focused on the half-dragon with silver hair and smoke gray eyes.

"Char," she breathed in surprise.

Levet gave a click of his tongue. "How many dragons do you possess, *ma belle?*"

Char moved to peer down at the gargoyle who pressed close to her side.

"Do you want me to kill the lump?" he asked.

Tayla gave a sharp shake of her head. She might have assumed he was kidding if she hadn't just witnessed him lopping off the head of a troll.

"No."

Levet took a step forward, his wings quivering with outrage.

"Lump?" He thumped his chest with a small fist. "I am Levet, the greatest—"

"Not now, Levet," Tayla gently interrupted.

She adored the gargoyle, but he could go on for hours about his heroic deeds.

Char gave a shake of his head, as if he couldn't believe she wouldn't want her companion dead, then held out a slender hand.

"We need to get out of here. Can you create a portal?"

She slowly straightened, struggling to keep her balance as the shaking continued.

"What about Baine?" she demanded.

Char shrugged, showing an astonishing lack of concern for his master.

"He'll continue to distract the bastards until we're out of here," he said, keeping a tight grip on her hand. "We need to go."

"We can't leave him behind," she protested. "What if he gets hurt?"

Char snorted. "He's a big boy. Trust me, he can take care of himself."

She gave a grudging nod. There were few things that could actually pose a danger to a dragon.

Still, she couldn't leave. Not yet.

"What about my father?"

Char studied her with rising frustration. "Unless you want the pleasure of killing him with your own hands, I'm sure the assassins will dispose of him once they realize he's of no use."

"No," she protested. "I don't want him dead."

Char studied her with a baffled expression. "Why not?"

"My precise question," Levet muttered.

"Shut up," Char growled, his gaze never leaving Tayla.

"Hey," Levet protested.

Tayla heaved a small sigh. She'd never make anyone understand.

"I can't just leave him here."

For a tense moment, Tayla thought the dragon might force her out of the tunnel. It wasn't like she was strong enough to fight him if he decided to toss her over his shoulder and leave the castle.

Then, clearly sensing she would blame him if anything happened to Odel, he turned to tug her through the darkness.

"Baine is going to kill me..."

CHAPTER TWELVE

With long strides, Craven moved through his castle that was being methodically destroyed by the dragon flying overhead. Somewhere in his thick skull he knew he should be terrified. No one faced off against a dragon and lived to tell the tale. But it was fury that thundered through him as he stepped onto the rampart to discover Reece staring at the sky in horror.

Craven's eyes flashed with crimson as he followed his companion's gaze toward the massive creature that was belching fire. He hissed in fury. With each blast the bastard was turning the castle's outer fortifications into smoldering piles of rubble.

"Shit," he growled, watching as his five-million-dollar investment went up in smoke. "Does he have to destroy the whole damned place? I spent a fortune on this lair." His hands clenched. "Not to mention the spells that are supposed to protect it. I'm going to kill that witch."

The smaller male shoved back his long hair with fingers that visibly trembled.

"There's not a witch in the world who has magic strong enough to keep out dragon-fire," Reece muttered. "Maybe you shouldn't have provoked the flying lizard."

"Me? Don't you mean 'we'?" Craven growled, his heavy boots scraping against the stones beneath his feet as he lurched to the side. Damn the dragon and his blasts of fire. The entire place was shaking as if there was an earthquake. "We're in this together."

Reece shrugged, lifting a slender hand. "Sorry, but I'm sure you've heard the old saying that 'there's no honor among thieves' and all that crap. Especially when there's a dragon involved." He waved his hand. Then, waved it again, and again. His eyes widened with fear. "Oh…hell."

Craven smirked. "Problems?"

"I can't form a portal," the fairy mongrel breathed in shock.

Craven arched a brow. He'd specifically had the witch cast her spell so it recognized the fairy's magic.

"Don't look at me," he said. "I have no ability to alter the spell."

Reece glanced toward the sky. "The dragon must have blanketed us with his magic."

"A pity." Turning on his heel, Craven headed back toward the door.

He'd vaguely hoped he would come up here to discover the spells he'd paid out the ass to have wrapped around his property would be protecting them from the dragon attack. Now it was obvious the only option was to flee.

Not surprisingly, Reece was on his heels as he headed down the narrow flight of stairs.

"Where are you going?" Reece squawked, clearly forgetting his claim of every thief for himself.

"Unlike you, I actually planned for an emergency," Craven informed him.

The fairy released a shaky sigh, the scent of his fear filling the air.

"You have a way out?"

Craven grimaced as he continued down the spiral staircase. He wanted to grab Reece by the throat and toss him out one of the narrow windows. Watching the treacherous fairy being burnt to a crisp might ease a portion of his seething frustration. Unfortunately, he couldn't deny that the male had his uses.

Once they left the castle and were away from the dragon's smothering magic, they would need a quick escape out of the mountains. What better way than a handy dandy portal?

He could use the imp, of course. But, he couldn't be sure she wouldn't double-cross him.

No. For now, he had little choice but to allow Reece to tag along.

He swallowed a low snarl of annoyance, reassuring himself that he could always kill the idiotic fairy after he was safely away from the dragon.

"Yes, I have a way out," he admitted, wincing as a shower of rocks tumbled from the ceiling to bounce off his head. "But first I have to go to the dungeons."

Reece jerked to the side, blood running down his forehead from a stray rock.

"Why?"

"That's where I left the imp."

Reece wiped the blood from his face. "An unfortunate casualty of war."

"Bullshit," Craven snarled. "I've waited twenty years to get my hands on the bitch. There's no way in hell I'm leaving without her."

"In case you missed the memo, we're being attacked by an angry dragon," Reece snapped.

Craven rolled his eyes. Yeah, like he could miss the fact the castle was crumbling around him? Or the stench of melting metal? Or the shrill death cries from the trolls who were trying to flee the destruction?

"Then leave," he told his companion.

"Where's your emergency exit?"

Craven halted to yank open the heavy iron door that blocked the end of the staircase. Then, with a smile, he stepped to the side and waved Reece to go ahead of him.

"Follow me and I'll show you."

"Shit." Reece peered into the dark tunnel that led to the dungeons before glancing over his shoulder at the stairs that were splitting beneath the impact of the dragon strikes. "I didn't sign up for this," he complained.

Craven snorted. "You thought it would be easy to steal a priceless hoard?"

Reece's expression hardened with reproach. "You promised we'd be in and out before anyone realized we were there."

Craven shrugged. It should have been that simple. He still didn't know how the dragon had found him. Or why he was currently destroying the castle.

Unless he knew the imp was there and was trying to kill her?

"That was the plan," he muttered.

"What's the plan now?"

Craven made a sound of impatience. "Get the imp and wait until the heat is off. Literally."

Reece gave a sharp, humorless laugh. "You think the dragons are ever going to stop hunting you if they know you have a way to sneak into their lairs?"

Did he? Craven muttered a curse. Of course didn't. If they suspected he was plotting to steal their hoards, the dragons wouldn't stop until he was dead.

He glared at his companion. "What do you suggest?"

"Forget the imp and get the hell out of here," Reece promptly suggested.

"And what about the treasure?"

"You'd be alive." Reece deliberately touched the gash that was rapidly healing on his brow. "Sometimes that's the greatest treasure of all."

Okay, the fairy had point. Craven might be greedy, but he wasn't willing to die to get his hands on a hoard. Still, the thought of leaving behind the female he'd spent so much time and money to track down was grating against his nerves.

"I…" Craven allowed his words to trail away, a sudden fear twisting his gut at the thick silence that filled the air. "Listen," he hissed.

"What?" Reece's brows snapped together. "I don't hear anything."

"That's the point, you moron." Craven reached for the gun he had holstered at his lower back. Not that it was going to do him a damn bit of good. Human technology was worthless against the more powerful demons. "Where's the dragon?"

There was a sizzle of electric energy as a portal opened and a slender, dark-haired man appeared on the stairs. For a crazed second, Craven tried to convince himself it was a fey who'd managed to break through the barriers. Then, he caught sight of the fire that blazed in the amber eyes and he knew he was dead.

"Were you looking for me?" the dragon drawled, allowing his power to roar through the air.

"Oh…shit," Craven breathed, scrambling backward, nearly tripping over Reece in an effort to get away.

But it was too late.

Far too late.

Slowly the dragon lifted his hand, whispering a word of power. Craven screamed as a ball of flame slammed into him, the heat searing him to his very bones.

Tayla hurried through the dark tunnels, well aware of the two males who prowled directly behind her.

The half-breed dragon and miniature gargoyle couldn't be more different, but they managed to express mutual vibes of annoyed disapproval. Was it something males practiced?

They were very good at it.

Refusing to be distracted, Tayla turned down another tunnel that was lined with thick doors. Some were made out of iron, some silver, and one was made out of pure stone. Obviously her captor liked to be prepared for whatever species of demon he might feel in the mood to lock up.

Following the scent of figs, she came to a halt at the last door that was made of iron.

Instantly she could hear the sound of her father's desperate voice.

"Hello. Can you hear me? I'm trapped." There was pounding on the opposite side of the door. "I know there's someone out there. Help me and I can pay you," Odel lowered his voice, no doubt hoping to wheedle a deal with the guards. "I have money. Jewels. Anything you want."

Char made a sound of disgust. "He's very noisy," he complained. "I could remove his tongue."

"No," Tayla retorted, fairly certain that the dragon wasn't teasing.

Levet waddled to stand at her side. "Are you certain, *ma belle*? The dragon has a point."

She scowled down at her companion. "No."

Levet gave a flap of his wings, glancing toward Char. "I tried."

There was more banging on the door. "Who's there?" her father demanded. "Tayla? My sweet Tay-Tay, is that you?"

Tayla stiffened. Once upon a time her father's nickname for her would have warmed her heart. It didn't matter that he was constantly on the run, or that they never had money, or that he often forgot her for days on end. She'd told herself that as long as they were together, they were a family.

Now there was a stark emptiness in the center of her heart.

Stepping forward, she spoke directly through the tiny slot carved into the door. She assumed it was there so a guard could keep a constant watch on the prisoner if necessary.

"I'm here, father," she assured the older imp.

"Oh, thank the gods." Odel gave a rough sob. Despite his habit of flaunting the law, and gambling away money he didn't have, her father was terrified of confined places. Perhaps because he was often threatened with being locked in a room and having the key thrown away. "I knew you would come for me."

Tayla grimaced, glancing toward the dragon standing in the center of the tunnel, his stormy eyes searching for any hint of trouble.

"Can you open the door?" she asked.

Char turned to study her with a frown, looking as if he wanted to refuse her request. Then, seeing the grim determination that was etched on her face, he threw his hands up in resignation.

"Yes, I can open the damned door," he growled. With gentle care he tugged her to the side, before shouting at her father. "Stand back, you idiot." Lifting his leg, he gave a massive kick that smashed the door off its hinges and sent it flying through the air to smack against the back wall. He glanced toward a wide-eyed Tayla. "There. It's open."

"Thank you," she squeaked, darting into the cell and shuddering at the sight of the door that was now a twisted pile of iron.

Yow. She'd think twice before asking Char for help again.

Odel rushed forward, grasping her fingers in a tight grip. Although he was unharmed by the carnage, he looked decidedly worse for wear. His hair was tangled as if it hadn't been brushed in days, and his eyes bloodshot from weeks of consuming human alcohol. Worse, he smelled as if he hadn't bothered to bathe in recent memory.

"Oh, my dear girl, you can't believe how happy I am to see you," he gushed, his grip so tight it hurt her fingers.

Her lips twisted into a sad smile. "Are you?"

He frowned, sensing her wary disbelief. "Of course."

She tugged her hands free, trying not to notice how pathetic he looked in his wrinkled clothing and the streaks of dust on his cheek.

Odel was a master at playing on her sympathy, but this time she wasn't in the mood for his games. He'd wounded her too deeply.

"Because I can be of use, isn't that right?" she asked. "That's the only time you bother to notice I'm alive."

He placed a hand to his chest, as if he was the one hurt. "How could you say that, Tayla?"

"How?" She wrapped her arms around her waist, glaring at the male who should have devoted his life to protecting her. "You sold me."

He at least had the grace to flinch at her sharp accusation.

"No," he breathed. "It wasn't like that at all."

Her jaw tightened as she recalled the night she'd been attacked by the trolls. Her father had deliberately left her alone in the store, offering her up to the trolls like some sacrificial lamb.

"Then you didn't use me to pay your debts?"

"I..." With a low groan, Odel fell to his knees, his head bent as he covered his face in his hands. "I'm sorry," he muttered, the words muffled. "I had to do something. They were going to kill me."

Focused on her father, Tayla nearly jumped out of her skin when Char brushed a gentle hand over her shoulder.

"We don't have time for this."

The dragon was right. They were in the dungeons of a...well, she wasn't entirely sure what Craven was, but she did know he was evil. Baine was risking himself to give them time to escape. The longer she remained, the more danger she put him in.

But even as she told herself to turn and leave the cell, she was sending Char a pleading glance.

"I need to know why," she said in husky tones.

The dragon gave a tense nod. "Five minutes."

Tayla returned her attention to the imp who had lifted his head to regard her with a wary gaze.

"I knew you were helpless and utterly self-centered, but I thought you loved me," she accused.

"I do." He looked stricken that she would even question his devotion. "I love you with all my heart, Tayla."

"But you love gambling more."

He started to shake his head, only to heave a resigned sigh. They both knew she'd been barely more than an afterthought when he was being consumed by his madness.

"I wasn't always this weak, wretched male, Tayla," he said in a mere whisper.

Char rolled his eyes, folding his arms over his chest. "Here comes the sob story."

"True that," Levet said, lifting his hand as if expecting the dragon to give him a high five. When Char simply glared at him, Levet blew him a raspberry. "It is rude to leave a gargoyle hanging."

"It's not a story," Odel insisted, ignoring the two males who regarded him with blatant disgust. "Once I was young and handsome, and so talented that I was the envy of my tribe." His shoulders straightened, his head tilting back as he remembered the days of his glory. "There wasn't a male who could brew a more potent nectar. Or charm more females to his bed."

Tayla held up a hand. "Not what I want to hear."

"I'm just saying that I was destined to succeed, no matter what I might choose to do with my life. Which is why no one was surprised when your mother chose me as her partner."

"Why would anyone be surprised?" she asked. Although fey often had arranged matings, it wasn't unusual for a male and female to choose one another based on love.

"Because she was a Chantri," he said. "She could have had any male she wanted."

Tayla's mouth dropped open. Odel rarely spoke of her mother. And since it was obviously painful for the older imp to speak about the female he'd loved and lost, Tayla hadn't wanted to press for information.

Now she felt as if she'd been blindsided.

"Chantri?" she repeated, trying to wrap her head around the idea. "My mother was a royal?"

"Yes." Seemingly unaware that he'd just dropped a bombshell, Odel gave a short nod. "A few stayed behind when the king returned with the purebloods to the fairy homeland. Arrita preferred the freedom of this world to being locked in paradise," he said.

"That explains it," Levet murmured.

Tayla glanced at the gargoyle in confusion. "Explains what?"

"Your ability to create portals in a dragon's lair," Levet said. "A few of the more powerful Chantri can open portals anywhere. Even open more than one portal at a time."

Without warning, Odel surged to his feet. "You have your mother's talent?" he said with sudden excitement. He'd never paid close enough attention to know what she could or couldn't do. "Can you really enter a...arrgg—" His words were choked off as Char reached out and grasped him by the throat, lifting him five inches off the ground. Odel's eyes protruded, his face turning a strange shade of puce. "Shit, Tayla," her father rasped. "Call off your boy."

She met Char's stormy gaze before giving a slow shake of her head.

"No," she firmly refused.

Odel made a strangled sound. "What do you mean, no?"

"Do you think I'm stupid?" she demanded. "You're already scheming how to use my talent for your own profit." She watched the guilt darken his eyes. "I'm warning you right now, I won't do it. Not for any reason."

Char snorted, a tendril of smoke escaping his flared nostrils.

"Don't worry, babe," he drawled, leaning forward until he could stare directly into her father's eyes. "Baine will kill him before he allows this creature to put you in danger."

There was something in the male's flat voice that warned them all he wasn't exaggerating. For Tayla, Baine would destroy Odel without hesitation.

The puce shade of his face paled to an ashen hue. "I won't," he choked out. "I swear."

Tayla reached out to lightly touch Char's forearm. "Let him down."

The male scowled. "You're kind of a buzzkill," he muttered, obviously disappointed he wasn't going to get to do something nasty to her father. "Fine."

Tayla waited until the male had dropped Odel back to his feet before stepping between the two. She'd discovered enough about dragons to know they had a quick temper and were eager to torch their enemies.

She didn't know if Char had dragon-fire, but it seemed wise to avoid any unfortunate 'accidents.'

"You were telling me about my mother," she reminded her father.

The older imp staggered as he tried to keep his balance. With his jaw clenched in anger, he kept his attention locked on Tayla. He was smart enough not to say anything to provoke the half-breed dragon. Char was just waiting for an excuse to rip out his tongue.

"She was beautiful, like you. And so gentle. Like a delicate flower." An achingly sad smile touched his lips. "All I ever wanted was to keep her close and protect her."

Pain clenched her heart. It didn't matter that she couldn't remember the female who'd given birth to her. Tayla still mourned her loss.

"Instead the vampires killed her," she murmured.

"Yes." Their gazes locked, silently sharing their mutual sorrow. "The knowledge that I failed her is like a cancer that is eating at my soul," Odel continued in harsh tones. "I constantly search for some way to dull the agony."

Tayla blinked in confusion. It'd never occurred to her that her father felt guilt at her mother's death.

"It wasn't your fault," she said. Arrita wasn't the only imp killed during the leeches' bloody spree through New England. "No one knew vampires were in the area, hunting fey."

Odel hunched his shoulders. "It doesn't matter," he muttered. "Without your mother I'm a broken male."

A mixture of sympathy and annoyance at her father's habit of wallowing in self-pity surged through Tayla, but even as her lips parted to tell him to man up, she felt the ground shake beneath her feet.

She frowned, abruptly realizing that it was the first mini earthquake she'd felt in several minutes. What had Baine been doing? Had he been injured?

Almost as if he shared her concern, Char closed his eyes, his expression distracted. Tayla held her breath. She'd heard rumors that dragons could communicate telepathically. Several seconds passed, then without warning, the male reached out to grasp her arm.

"We have to go," he said, his tone warning he wasn't going to argue.

Her heart squeezed with fear. "Is he okay?"

"Yeah." The male grimaced. "But he's going apeshit waiting to know you're safe. If we don't get out of here he's coming to get you himself."

A ridiculous glow of warmth filled her soul. The magnificent, glorious dragon was worried about her.

"I'm ready." She lifted her hand to create the portal, only to hesitate. "Where should we go?"

Char sent her a baffled glance. "Home, of course."

"You mean Baine's lair?"

Reaching out, Char brushed his fingers down her cheek. "That's what I said...home."

Slicing her hand through the air, Tayla led her odd collection of companions into Baine's throne room. She told herself that the sense of peace was nothing more than relief that they'd all managed to survive.

But even as she glanced around the elegant chamber, Char's word whispered through the back of her mind.

Home...

CHAPTER THIRTEEN

Baine didn't kill his friend. Char was, after all, a valuable companion.

But it was a close thing.

He'd actually been in a good mood when he'd returned to his private lair. Char had sent word that Tayla was safe and Baine had been able to release his smoldering frustration on the unfortunate assassins and band of trolls.

He'd made the ground shake, he'd spewed fire, and he'd created havoc among the natives.

Three of his favorite things.

By the time he'd left, the castle had been a smoking ruin and the bastards who had been hunting Tayla were dead. Or at least he assumed they were dead.

If any had escaped they now understood that Baine would destroy anyone who attempted to harm his mate.

But he'd barely had time to shift into his human form when his trusted servant entered the library of his private rooms to inform Baine that he'd had no choice but to rescue Tayla's father.

Shoving his fingers through his dark hair, Baine glared at the smirking Char. The younger male clearly found humor in the thought of Baine being stuck with the worthless imp.

It made Baine want to kill something.

"What the hell am I supposed to do with him?" Baine snarled.

"I don't know." Char gave a lift of his hands, his overly innocent expression scraping against Baine's temper. "He's your in-law, not mine."

"If you'd left him with the trolls—"

"Not my call," Char interrupted. "Your female insisted she wasn't leaving without him."

"Shit," Baine breathed.

He couldn't blame his servant. For such a small demon, Tayla had a talent for making a male rush to obey her commands. That didn't, however, ease his frustration.

It was bad enough to have that lump of cement she called a gargoyle in his lair. Now he had a drunken imp who would no doubt gamble away Baine's entire hoard if he weren't constantly guarded.

"You could always arrange an accident," Char suggested, his lips twitching as the scent of lemons filled the air just seconds before Tayla stepped into the room.

Wearing a soft cashmere sweater and gray slacks, she should have looked prim and prissy. The sort of female who would be horrified by the lustful urges of a dragon.

Instead, the peach sweater emphasized the luscious swell of her breasts, and the slacks clung to the rounded curve of her ass.

"What sort of accident?" she demanded as she strolled forward, her pale green eyes wary.

Baine waved a hand toward Char, his gaze never leaving Tayla as he inwardly debated how swiftly he could get her out of those prim clothes and stretched naked on his bed.

Primitive, but hey, he was a dragon.

"Leave us," he growled.

"As you command, my lord." Char performed a deep, mocking bow before turning to head across the floor. He paused next to Tayla to whisper loudly in her ear. "Give him hell, darling."

Baine shook his head as his servant at last strolled out of the room, closing the door behind him.

"He needs a mate," he muttered.

Tayla stood near one of the bookshelves, trying to look like she hadn't been startled by his words. "I thought dragons rarely mated?"

Baine moved forward. Enough with the games. He intended to claim her, once and for all.

"It's not as common as among some species, but it's not exactly rare." He halted directly in front of her. "Tayla—"

"I suppose you're angry that I left?" she hastily interrupted, her cheeks flushed.

Baine narrowed his gaze. "I'm angry that you put yourself in danger," he corrected.

She bit her bottom lip. "I couldn't leave Levet and my father in trouble."

Baine shuddered at the thought of what might have happened if he hadn't sensed her leaving the lair. The assassins would have fed her to the trolls...

With an effort he slammed shut the door on his darkest fears. He couldn't even let himself think of losing this female.

"We'll deal with those two idiots later," he muttered.

"But—"

Her words ended on a squeak as he leaned down to scoop her off her feet.

"Later," he insisted, cradling her against his chest as he moved to walk through a doorway that was carefully hidden behind a weave of illusion.

Instantly they were stepping into a cavernous room that was fit for a sultan.

A large round bed stood in the center of a mosaic-tiled floor, draped in black and gold bedding. There was a deep bath in one corner that was bigger than most swimming pools, and in another corner was a pile of pillows where he could relax and read without worry that he might be interrupted.

"Where are you taking me?" Tayla breathed.

"Where I should have taken you the second I saw you in my father's lair," he said, slowly lowering her to her feet.

She glanced around, her gaze lingering on the nearby bed before moving toward the priceless tapestries that hung on the walls.

"Good heavens."

He stroked his hand over her golden curls, needing to touch her. He'd released a portion of his fury during his destruction of the assassins' castle, but he was still working through his terror that he might lose her.

That was going to take some time.

"You're the first person ever to enter my private sleeping chamber," he told her.

She blinked, as if startled by his confession. "Why me?"

His fingers slid beneath her hair so he could discover the tender skin of her nape.

"You know why."

He could hear her heart begin to race, a flush staining her cheeks.

"You said I belong with your hoard," she muttered.

Baine grimaced with regret. Being an all-powerful dragon didn't keep him from acting like an idiot on occasion.

"Because you pissed me off," he admitted.

She shivered as his fingers lightly traced the neckline of her sweater.

"I didn't mean to."

He leaned down, capturing her guarded gaze. "Yes, you did. You were frightened by the intensity of your response to me. So you panicked and tried to put barriers between us."

She lowered her lashes, as if she could pretend he hadn't guessed exactly why she'd been so anxious to push him away.

"Arrogant," she muttered.

"I am," he readily agreed. "Which is why I allowed you to manipulate me into putting space between us." He moved close enough to feel the soft cashmere rubbing against his bare chest. "Something that will never happen again." His thumb pressed against the pulse that hammered at the base of her throat. "Especially now that I know about your little trick."

She licked her lips, her eyes darkening. But it wasn't fear. No. He could smell the heady scent of her arousal beginning to waft through the air.

"I promise I won't take off again," she said, her voice husky. "Not until I'm released from your debt."

His brows snapped together, his fingers dipping beneath the neckline of her sweater to tug out the delicate golden chain he'd placed there what seemed like an eternity ago.

"There is no debt." With one small burst of power he destroyed the dragon marque.

She glanced down in shock, her hand lifting as if she actually missed the narrow chain.

"What are you saying?"

"I absolve you of any obligation," he told her. There would be no more excuses for her to hide behind when he held her in his arms. "You are free."

She slowly tilted back her head to meet his brooding gaze. "I can leave?"

He clenched his teeth. Every instinct rebelled against giving her a choice. He was a dragon, dammit. He hoarded his treasures with a fierce, possessive jealousy.

But Tayla was more than just a precious bauble.

She was his mate.

And she had to choose her place at his side.

"If that's what you desire." He forced the words past his stiff lips, his hands unconsciously smoothing up and down her back while he allowed his heat to cloak around her. "But I hope very much you'll want to stay."

She instinctively arched toward him, a hint of vulnerability shimmering in her beautiful eyes.

"For how long?"

His answer came without hesitation. "Forever."

"Forever?" she breathed as she reached up to rest her hands on his broad chest. "That's a very long time."

Beneath her fingers she could feel the heat of his beast. Her smile widened. Was it possible she'd truly captured the heart of this magnificent creature?

"Not nearly long enough, when I've waited five centuries to at last discover you," he murmured. "Only to have you promptly disappear for another twenty-five years."

Her lips twitched at his disgruntled tone. He truly was disturbed by the fact that she'd managed to hide from him for so long.

"And what about your harem?" she demanded, stroking her fingers over his rigid muscles.

She thoroughly approved of his preference for going shirtless.

There were no barriers to stand between them. Nothing to halt her from exploring the silky warm skin and the fascinating tattoos that swirled over his body.

Approval rumbled deep in his chest as he reached to grab the hem of her sweater, smoothly tugging it over her head.

"What about it?" he asked in an absent voice, his jaw tightening and nose flaring as his gaze swept down to her bare breasts.

"I want it shut down."

His head lowered until she could feel his breath against her temple.

"Are you sure?"

Tiny sparks flowed through her blood as she used her nails to lightly scrape down his back.

"Do you intend to have other females?" she demanded.

He chuckled, a shudder shaking his body as her finger traced the waistband of his loose pants.

"Of course not, but it might be fun to play master and slave," he suggested in husky tones.

"I suppose you get to be the master?" she teased.

"Well, it was my suggestion," he said, a groan wrenched from his throat as she tugged the drawstring, allowing the pants to slide down his legs.

Instantly her fingers were wrapping around the hard length of his cock.

Although she'd already had more than one up-close and extremely personal encounter with Baine, she still felt a thrill of shock as she was reminded of the size of his cock.

And how hot it was to the touch.

Fascinated, she traced her fingers over the blunt tip and then down the shaft to the soft sack below.

"Hmm," she murmured. "I prefer the notion of having you kneeling at my feet."

"Holy hell," Baine moaned, his fingers closing over her own as he encouraged her to stroke up and down. "With this sort of incentive I promise I will kneel at your feet as often as you want."

"Promises, promises—"

Her mocking words broke off with a soft moan as he lowered his head and captured her lips in a fierce, demanding kiss.

White-hot need seared through her as she lifted her arms and wrapped them around his neck. Immediately the scent of exotic male spices filled the air.

Yum.

She shivered as his hands followed the curve of her spine, then cupped her butt in a possessive grip. His raw power filled her mind until there was nothing but him. The taste of his kiss, the incandescent heat of his touch.

Gently his tongue parted her lips to slip inside. Tayla eagerly opened to his caress. At the same time, Baine growled deep in his throat, allowing his hands to skim upward to at last cup the aching fullness of her breasts.

Tayla trembled. *Oh...yes.* She squeezed her eyes shut, savoring the sensation of his fingers teasing her nipples into tender peaks. Pleasure streaked through her body like bolts of lightning.

She pressed against his hard form, greedy for more.

"Baine."

His lips nuzzled her cheek as his thumbs continued to caress her aching nipples.

"I have been alone so long, Tayla," he whispered. "I never dared to hope I would ever have a mate."

The stark words sent a shiver of longing down her spine.

She better than anyone understood loneliness.

And a wistful yearning for a family that she kept tucked in a secret part of her heart.

"Your mate," she whispered.

"Mine." He pulled back to study her with a heated gaze. "Yes…mine at last."

The breath was knocked from her lungs as he reached down to scoop her off her feet, and moved into the shadows of the vast bedroom. Tayla had never felt so protected as she did in his strong arms, and she turned her head to nuzzle the bare skin of his chest.

This was what it meant to share her life with another, she hazily acknowledged.

Clutching his shoulders she sensed as Baine slowly lowered her onto the pillows of the wide bed. She lifted her heavy lashes to watch as he hastily reached down to jerk off her shoes and then wrestle her out of the remainder of her clothing. There was none of his usual grace but somehow his obvious impatience only increased the excitement that thundered through her body.

He was so…beautiful.

A magnificent combination of hard muscles, sinew, and raw power that would make any female shiver in anticipation.

Expecting Baine to join her on the mattress, Tayla was caught off guard when he bent beside the bed, a wicked smile tugging at his lips.

"You said you wanted me on my knees."

Her heart missed a beat. *Oh yeah.* Having this gorgeous male as her sex slave was a fantasy she was going to relish for several centuries.

Maybe a few millennia.

"Do you always intend to be so accommodating?" she teased.

He leaned forward to hover just above her waiting mouth.

"Probably not. I'm usually an opinionated ass."

She rolled her eyes. "I'm not going to argue with that."

"I didn't think you would." Skimming his mouth over her parted lips, Baine pulled back to watch as his fingers drifted down the slope of her shoulder and under the curve of her breast. His eyes smoldered with amber fire as she trembled in reaction. "You're so beautiful," he whispered. "Perfect."

Her breath hissed between her teeth as he lightly circled her straining nipples in a teasing motion.

"Baine."

With a husky growl Baine lowered his head to capture the tip of her breast in his mouth. Tayla cried out in pleasure as she arched upward. Over and over his tongue tormented the hardened nub as he used his erotic skill to drive her to the edge of madness.

Tayla clenched her teeth, her brain shutting down as a molten heat flowed through her veins.

Not that it mattered.

Who wanted to think when they could feel?

Teasing her nipple with growing insistence, Baine trailed his fingers down the quivering muscles of her stomach. With exquisite care he explored every inch of her satin skin, circling her belly button and drifting over her thighs.

Tayla bit her lower lip. He was deliberately tormenting her. Clearly enjoying the sight of her writing beneath his touch. But any words of protest remained locked in her throat. Her entire body might be coiled tight with an eager desire to climax, but she was as anxious as Baine to prolong this moment.

This was her mate. The male who was entwined with her very soul.

As if capable of reading her mind, Baine stroked his lips over the curve of her breast before tracing the line of her collarbone. Then, whispering a soft word of power, he released a burst of magic.

Tayla felt a golden heat race over her skin. Opening her eyes, she glanced down to discover that the dragon marque was once again around her neck. Only this time it wasn't a gold chain, but instead a brilliant strand of amber that glowed with the same fire as in Baine's eyes.

"What is it?" she breathed in amazement.

"A mating sacrament." His lips gently brushed over the precious stones. "My promise that you are a gift I will always cherish."

Joy radiated through her body.

Mate.

Her mate.

Twining her fingers through the softness of his hair, Tayla urged Baine up so she could kiss him with all the love that flooded through her heart.

He readily returned the kiss, his fingers stroking as light as a butterfly wing along the line of her cleft.

Tayla jerked in pleasure.

"I need you now, Baine," she rasped.

He lifted his head and their gazes collided. In the shadows his features were impossibly beautiful, his expression tense with raw desire.

Slowly he moved onto the bed, his solid weight pressing her into the mattress. Then, sliding his hands beneath her thighs, he tugged her legs apart so he could settle between them. The sensation of his hot skin pressed against her sent a rush of excitement through her.

It felt so utterly right as he cradled his hips even deeper, his chest rubbing her aching nipples. As if he somehow completed her.

Running her hands down his back, Tayla savored the hard muscles that rippled beneath her touch. He was a lethal predator who could rule the world.

And yet he treated her as if she was his most priceless treasure.

She smiled as she shivered beneath him. This was why his touch ignited the fire within her. Why she ached for his kisses.

It wasn't just his raw, masculine perfection. Or his skilled caresses. It was the knowledge deep in her heart that his loyalty was absolute.

He would never abandon her, never betray her, and never, ever stop caring about her.

Heady stuff for a female who'd never been truly loved.

Her hands reached the smooth curve of his butt and Tayla felt him shudder as she cupped him with restless desire.

His hooded gaze swept over her face before he was leaning down to stroke his lips over her forehead.

"Tell me this mating is what you desire, Tayla," he demanded. "Tell me you want to be mine forever."

She reached up to frame his face in her hands. "Forever, my love."

"My love," he echoed, the aching tenderness in his voice nearly bringing tears to her eyes.

A shiver racked his body as his lips brushed over her flushed features.

"My heart beats for you," he murmured, his words a soft pledge. "There is no going back for either of us."

His breath seared over her skin as he tilted his hips to press the tip of his cock against her entrance.

She moaned in pleasure as his erection relentlessly pressed deeper into her damp heat, stretching her to the point of near pain.

Delicious.

Muttering beneath his breath, Baine pulled out before he was shoving forward, impaling her with one smooth thrust.

"Yes," she groaned, wrapping her legs around his hips.

Buried deep inside her, Baine trailed his mouth over her skin to at last kiss her with a devouring hunger.

At the same time, he began to rock softly against her. With each thrust his tongue stroked into her mouth, the matching rhythm intensifying the furious pleasure that spread through her body.

Her fingers flexed as a whimper lodged in her throat. The sheer intimacy of having him balls-deep inside her was intensified by the white flames that danced over their bodies. The dragon-fire entwined them, a physical display of their mating.

His breath rasped in the shadowed silence as he quickened his pace.

"Never leave me again," he muttered against her lips. "I need to know you'll be here with me."

Dear lord, it was too much. She felt as if she was going to explode into a billion tiny pieces.

She scored her nails down his back, the pleasure almost unbearable.

"Always..." she moaned.

"My beautiful imp," he whispered, his head lowering to take her breast in his mouth.

Using his teeth and tongue he tormented her tight nipple, the blaze of sensations spiraling to a critical point.

Her breath was shattered as he gave a last, violent surge and tossed her over the edge into a whirlwind of pulsing bliss.

Her soft scream mingled with his low groan of completion as he slumped on top of her, both of them lost in a fog of transcendental joy.

Time passed, a second or an eternity, before Baine rolled to his side and pulled her into his arms. With a sigh Tayla rested her head on his chest, floating on a sense of wonderment.

"My mate," he whispered as he nuzzled her ear.

Tayla smiled, ignoring the flames that continued to dance over his skin as she brushed her lips over his chest.

"I like when you play sex slave, my lord," she teased. "I think we'll keep the harem."

His arms tightened as he seared a path of dragon-kisses down the curve of her neck.

"Your wish, sweet Tayla, is my command."

CHAPTER FOURTEEN

It wasn't easy to stun a five-hundred-year-old dragon.
But making love to Tayla had shaken Baine to his very
soul.

Who knew that the feel of her slender body pressed
against him would release his dragon-fire until the sheets
were scorched and Tayla's ivory skin rosy from the
intense heat? Or that he would feel the most unexpected
urge to cry at the mere thought that this female would
now be forever bound to him?

So it was no surprise that the last thing Baine wanted
was to leave his bed where he had a naked Tayla
wrapped in his arms.

Unfortunately, he'd put off dealing with his ruthless
father long enough.

Synge might be a cunning hunter who understood
the need for patience, but he wasn't going to wait

forever. Sooner or later he would make his move to get his hands on Tayla.

Probably sooner.

Which was why he'd forced himself to urge Tayla to dress while he pulled on his pants and called for Char to bring Fist to the throne room.

Now he sat on his massive chair with Tayla standing beside him, once again prim and proper in her sweater and pearls. In silence, he studied the male who was kneeling at his feet.

Fist had his head bent as he mentally sent the message that Baine had commanded.

At last, the younger male glanced up to meet Baine's fierce glare.

"You managed to contact Synge?" he demanded.

Fist nodded. The days in the dungeon hadn't been particularly kind to the onetime soldier. He looked thinner, with dark circles beneath his eyes.

But he was still alive, which was more than he deserved.

"Yes, my lord," Fist assured him. "He believes you're getting ready to start the auction for the imp."

"Good." Baine ignored Tayla's tiny gasp as he nodded toward Char who was standing directly behind Fist. "Take him back to the dungeons and then wait for my signal. Once I have Synge's agreement I'll need you to handle the details."

Char gave a nod, grabbing Fist by the back of his neck and hauling him roughly to his feet. Baine waited until the two males were out of the room before lifting his hand and making a slashing motion.

Instantly a portal formed.

Rising to his feet, he held out his hand. There was a momentary hesitation before Tayla moved to place her fingers against his palm. Swiftly Baine was tugging her into the portal, knowing she was already having second thoughts.

Understandable, considering he'd given her little information beyond the fact that they were meeting with his father.

Oh yeah, and the little FYI that Synge wanted her dead.

He'd decided to keep his hasty plan to himself. She was terrified enough, thank you very fucking much.

Stepping through the portal, they arrived in the back garden of Tayla's pretty Victorian house that was bathed in silver moonlight.

Inside Baine could hear the workers he'd sent earlier to clean and repair the damage caused by the trolls. Not that he intended for Tayla to return to this place. She belonged in the safety of his lair. But he knew it would trouble her to think that this home she'd created was falling into disrepair.

Stepping away as he released her hand, Tayla bit her bottom lip as she glanced toward the neatly trimmed rosebushes. No doubt she was thinking about the vast upheaval in her life.

That was one of the reasons he'd brought her here.

He needed her to say goodbye to her old life.

Only then would she be prepared to accept their future together.

"Are you sure this is going to work?" she muttered.

"Trust me," he assured her, resisting the urge to wrap her in his arms.

He wanted to be in a position to fight off any attacks.

He better than anyone knew that danger lurked in the shadows.

"You I trust," she said in low tones. "But your father..." She wrapped her arms around her waist, shivering with a fear she couldn't disguise. "You said yourself that he wants to kill me."

Flames flickered over Baine's bare chest before he controlled his burst of anger. No one was hurting Tayla. No matter who he had to destroy.

"Not after I speak with him," he swore.

Her eyes widened as a burst of heat swept through the garden.

"I think he's here," she breathed.

Baine moved to stand in front of her as his father stepped out of a portal.

"Stay close," he muttered.

"Don't worry." Tayla pressed a hand to his lower back, as if needing the reassurance of touching him.

A bone-deep happiness raced through him. He didn't want her frightened. Hell, it infuriated him to think she would know even a second of fear. But there was something intensely satisfying in the knowledge she would depend on him for comfort.

With cautious steps, the large male moved toward Baine, his brutish features hard with determination.

"Welcome, sire," Baine murmured.

The silver gaze narrowed as Synge's attention turned toward the house where the sound of hammering echoed through the air.

"What's going on here?"

"I'm assisting Tayla in repairing her home."

Synge sent him a puzzled frown. "Tayla?"

Baine stepped aside to reveal the female standing behind him.

"Tayla, allow me to formally present you to my father, Synge."

"Hello," Tayla murmured in tentative tones, unaware of the importance of Baine's words.

The older dragon, however, was very conscious of what Baine was saying. With a scowl he folded his arms over his massive chest, refusing to acknowledge Baine's claim.

"Where are the others?" he instead demanded.

Baine arched a brow. "What others?"

Synge made a sound of impatience. "I heard there was to be an auction among the trolls tonight."

"Ah yes, the trolls," Baine drawled. It was childish, but he couldn't deny he was enjoying tormenting his father. "I'm afraid they can't make it."

"Why not?"

Baine shrugged. "Because I killed them."

"Good." The silver gaze flicked toward Tayla. "It should make the auction a lot less complicated."

Baine deliberately moved to block Tayla from his father's sight. It was a silent warning he would have to go through Baine to get to the female.

"Don't you want to know why they're dead?" he demanded.

"Not particularly." The ground shook as Synge stepped forward. "Name your price for the female."

Tayla pressed against his back, her breath brushing his bare skin as the tart scent of lemons filled the air.

"But I want to tell you," Baine insisted.

"Fine." The older male heaved an exaggerated sigh. "Why are they dead?"

"Because they were hunting my mate."

Synge clenched his hands at his side, bluish sparks dancing over his body.

"Your mate?" Synge pretended he didn't know exactly what Baine was saying. "You found her?"

"I did." Reaching behind him, Baine tugged Tayla to his side, wrapping a possessive arm around her shoulders. The game had been fun, but now it was time to end it.

The flames danced higher, heating the air. "This imp?"

Baine growled low in his throat. "Her name is Tayla."

Synge waved aside the blatant reprimand. "You're sure?"

Baine gave a soft laugh, glancing toward the woman who'd captured his heart.

"It's like getting struck by lightning," he murmured. "It's not a sensation that a male makes a mistake about."

Synge ground his teeth. The older dragon had never chosen a consort, but like every other dragon had heard the stories of the unbreakable bond that was created during a mating.

"No, I suppose not," he at last conceded.

"Do you accept my formal introduction?" Baine demanded.

Synge narrowed his gaze. Tradition dictated that he accept his son's mate. But his fear for his hoard made him continue to battle against the inevitable.

"First you need to know something about her."

Baine leaned down to brush his lips over the top of Tayla's head.

"That she can create portals into a dragon lair?"

"You know?" Synge demanded in astonishment.

"I do."

"Then you realize she's a security risk," Synge growled.

Baine ran a comforting hand up and down Tayla's back as she gave a tiny shiver. His gaze, however, never wavered from his father.

It was a direct challenge.

"Not anymore," Baine said. "The trolls and their partners are dead."

Synge shook his head. "Even if you killed the trolls, that doesn't mean they didn't tell some other demon."

Baine allowed his power to flow from his body until the air was quivering with an unspoken threat.

"Do you truly think anyone would attempt to use my mate for any purpose?"

Synge took an unconscious step backward. "At least tell me you've discovered how she's able to do it."

Baine shrugged. "Her mother was a Chantri who was destroyed by vampires years ago."

Synge still wasn't satisfied. "Does she have any siblings?"

"None that inherited their mother's blood," Baine assured him.

At his side, Tayla rested her head against his arm. "And even if they had, they aren't anything like my father. They are all are hardworking fey with successful businesses and families."

"I can't wait to meet them, princess," Baine murmured.

He felt her stiffen. "Princess?"

He gave a low chuckle, enjoying the astonishment on her beautiful face.

"You do have royal blood," he reminded her, kissing the tip of her nose before returning his attention to the older male.

"Well, father?" he demanded.

There was a long pause before Synge offered a slow dip of his head.

"I accept that she's your mate."

Baine smiled. "Done."

"What does that mean?" Tayla asked.

"Dragons regularly battle other demons and even each other, but mates and the young are strictly protected," Baine explained, a sense of relief flooding through his body. Until his father had actually said the words, he couldn't be sure that Tayla would be safe. Now he knew beyond a doubt she would be guarded even if something happened to him. "It's our most sacred law. You're off-limits, no matter what happens." He paused, studying his father's grim expression. "Isn't that right, sire?"

"You win, Baine," his father conceded with a mocking salute. "This time."

Never a gracious loser, Synge turned to walk back into his waiting portal.

"Father." Baine halted him.

Synge glanced over his shoulder. "What?"

"You hold Fist's mate as a hostage."

"I do."

"I want her."

Speculation shimmered in the silver eyes. "It'll cost you."

"I never assumed otherwise," Baine retorted. "I've given Char permission to complete the negotiations."

Looking considerably happier now that he had the promise of reducing Baine's hoard by several treasure chests, Synge entered the portal and disappeared.

The peace of the night returned to the garden, and Tayla pulled away far enough to study his face with a hopeful expression.

"It's over?"

"Yes." He framed her face in his hands. "No one will dare try to take you from me."

A tremulous smile curved her lips, the moonlight shimmering over her golden hair. A sudden joy pierced his heart. This beautiful creature was his mate.

Now and forever.

"That was nice of you to help Fist," she murmured. "I thought you intended to keep him in the dungeons for betraying you."

He snorted, his fingers skimming down the curve of her throat, savoring the sensation of her satin skin.

"That's too easy."

"You think being locked in the dungeons is easy?" she inquired with a lift of her brows.

He shrugged. "I have a much better way to punish him."

She looked suddenly wary. "What are you going to do?"

"He's going to be responsible for keeping Odel out of trouble."

Tayla blinked. And then blinked again. "You're making him my father's babysitter?"

"Yes," Baine admitted without apology.

Fist had to be taught a lesson, and Baine could think of no worse penance than spending the next century trying to keep the drunken, gambling-addicted imp on the straight and narrow.

"That's..." Tayla abruptly released a low chuckle. "Diabolical."

"It's two problems solved," Baine said with a shrug, his nose wrinkling at the stench of granite that filled the air. Turning his head, he watched as the stunted gargoyle waddled out of the house and down the pathway into the garden. "Now only one to go," he muttered.

Tayla went on her tiptoes to press a kiss to Baine's tense jaw.

"Be nice," she chided, feeling giddy with happiness.

She'd not only gained a gorgeous, sexy dragon as a mate, but she was no longer being hunted. For the first time in twenty-five years she could breathe easy.

"I am," Baine growled, still glaring at the approaching gargoyle. "He's still alive, isn't he?"

Tayla rolled her eyes before she was spinning around to watch as Levet came to a halt next to her.

"*Ma belle*, the house will be lovely when it is completed," he said, his wings fluttering with enthusiasm. Tayla didn't blame him. The wood sprites were not only repairing the damage, but they'd built on a lovely conservatory that was filled with fresh herbs and flowers that could be grown year-round. "I cannot wait to once again taste your delicious scones."

Without warning, Baine's arm wrapped around her waist so he could tug her tight against his body.

"No one's going to be eating Tayla's scones from now on but me," he snarled.

"Baine," she breathed in protest, feeling a jolt of excitement at his touch.

Levet tilted his head to the side, studying her with open curiosity.

"Is this true?"

"I wouldn't put it in those exact words," Tayla said, making no effort to pull away from Baine's possessive grip. Why would she? This was precisely where she longed to be. "But I do plan to stay with Baine. I was hoping you would remain here and keep a watch on the house."

Levet's gray eyes widened in pleased surprise. "*Moi?*"

"Of course." She offered a gentle smile. This tiny demon had been a loyal friend, and regardless of Baine's less-than-complimentary opinion, Tayla would never forget his kindness.

"You do have a budding business to run," she pointed out.

"I do," he preened, puffing out his narrow chest. "But first I have a small duty to perform."

Tayla was almost afraid to ask. Sometimes Levet's duty could get him in serious trouble.

"What duty?"

"There is a young fairy in London who is waiting to be rescued. My days as KISA are not yet over." Reaching up, Levet grabbed Tayla's hand and pressed a brief kiss on her finger. "*Au revoir, ma belle.*"

193

Before Tayla could demand details, Levet was giving a flap of his fairy wings and heading toward the star-sprinkled sky.

"KISA?" Baine demanded as the gargoyle swiftly disappeared from view.

"Knight In Shining Armor," she explained with a small smile.

Baine snorted. "Let's go home."

"Yes," she breathed, her heart swelling with happiness.

Grasping her hand, he lifted her fingers to his lips, pressing a scorching kiss to her knuckles before he was urging her into his waiting portal.

They were briefly surrounded by a thick darkness before they were stepping out of the opening into Blaine's private bedroom. Instantly her tension eased.

Being in Baine's lair always made her feel safe.

Cherished…

And deliciously aroused.

Hopefully sensing her ready desire, Baine tugged her across the mosaic-tiled floor.

"I have a surprise for you," he murmured.

Tayla smiled as anticipation tingled through her body. "I don't suppose it includes your bed and…" Her words trailed away as she caught sight of the bag that was placed on the edge of the mattress. "My suitcase?"

Brushing his lips over her brow, he urged her forward. "Open it."

Slowly moving forward, she halted at the edge of the bed and lifted the top of the suitcase. Peering inside, she felt a stab of confusion.

"It's empty," she said.

"Exactly." Stepping forward, Baine reached to close the suitcase and shove it off the bed. Then, with gentle hands, he turned her to meet his smoldering gaze. "No more packed bags. No more escape plans. You're here to stay."

Her heart melted. He remembered.

Was it any wonder she loved him so desperately?

Holding his gaze, she wrapped her arms around his neck.

"Forever?"

He grasped her hips, tugging her against his stirring erection.

"Forever."

Tayla sighed in pleasure as Baine lowered his head to claim her lips in a kiss of searing demand.

After trying to avoid her fate for the past twenty-five years, she was done running. From this moment on, she was staying exactly where she belonged.

In the arms of her dragon…

THE END

KILL WITHOUT MERCY (ARES SECURITY)

BY ALEXANDRA IVY

PROLOGUE

Few people truly understood the meaning of 'hell on earth.'

The five soldiers who had been held in the Taliban prison in southern Afghanistan, however, possessed an agonizingly intimate knowledge of the phrase.

There was nothing like five weeks of brutal torture to teach a man that there are worse things than death.

It should have broken them. Even the most hardened soldiers could shatter beneath the acute psychological and physical punishment. Instead the torment only honed their ruthless determination to escape their captors.

In the dark nights they pooled their individual resources.

Rafe Vargas, a covert ops specialist. Max Grayson, trained in forensics. Hauk Laurensen, a sniper who was an expert with weapons. Teagan Moore, a computer wizard. And Lucas St. Clair, the smooth-talking hostage negotiator.

Together they forged a bond that went beyond friendship. They were a family bound by the grim determination to survive.

CHAPTER ONE

Friday nights in Houston meant crowded bars, loud music and ice-cold beer. It was a tradition that Rafe and his friends had quickly adapted to suit their own tastes when they moved to Texas five months ago.

After all, none of them were into the dance scene. They were too old for half-naked coeds and casual hookups. And none of them wanted to have to scream over pounding music to have a decent conversation.

Instead, they'd found The Saloon, a small, cozy bar with lots of polished wood, a jazz band that played softly in the background, and a handful of locals who knew better than to bother the other customers. Oh, and the finest tequila in the city.

They even had their own table that was reserved for them every Friday night.

Tucked in a back corner, it was shrouded in shadows and well away from the long bar that ran the length of one wall. A perfect spot to observe without being observed.

And best of all, situated so no one could sneak up from behind.

It might have been almost two years since they'd returned from the war, but none of them had forgotten. Lowering your guard, even for a second, could mean death.

Lesson. Fucking. Learned.

Tonight, however, it was only Rafe and Hauk at the table, both of them sipping tequila and eating peanuts from a small bucket.

Lucas was still in Washington D.C., working his contacts to help drum up business for their new security business, ARES. Max had remained at their new offices,

197

putting the final touches on his precious forensics lab, and Teagan was on his way to the bar after installing a computer system that would give Homeland Security a hemorrhage if they knew what he was doing.

Leaning back in his chair, Rafe intended to spend the night relaxing after a long week of hassling with the red tape and bullshit regulations that went into opening a new business, when he made the mistake of checking his messages.

"Shit."

He tossed his cellphone on the polished surface of the wooden table, a tangled ball of emotions lodged in the pit of his stomach.

Across the table Hauk sipped his tequila and studied Rafe with a lift of his brows.

At a glance, the two men couldn't be more different.

Rafe had dark hair that had grown long enough to touch the collar of his white button-down shirt along with dark eyes that were lushly framed by long, black lashes. His skin remained tanned dark bronze despite the fact it was late September, and his body was honed with muscles that came from working on the small ranch he'd just purchased, not the gym.

Hauk, on the other hand, had inherited his Scandinavian father's pale blond hair that he kept cut short, and brilliant blue eyes that held a cunning intelligence. He had a narrow face with sculpted features that were usually set in a stern expression.

And it wasn't just their outward appearance that made them so different.

Rafe was hot tempered, passionate and willing to trust his gut instincts.

Hauk was aloof, calculating, and mind-numbingly anal. Not that Hauk would admit he was OCD. He preferred to call himself detail-oriented.

Which was exactly why he was a successful sniper. Rafe, on the other hand, had been trained in combat rescue. He was capable of making quick decisions, and ready to change strategies on the fly.

"Trouble?" Hauk demanded.

Rafe grimaced. "The real estate agent left a message saying she has a buyer for my grandfather's house."

Hauk looked predictably confused. Rafe had been bitching about the need to get rid of his grandfather's house since the old man's death a year ago.

"Shouldn't that be good news?"

"It would be if I didn't have to travel to Newton to clean it out," Rafe said.

"Aren't there people you can hire to pack up the shit and send it to you?"

"Not in the middle of fucking nowhere."

Hauk's lips twisted into a humorless smile. "I've been in the middle of fucking nowhere, amigo, and it ain't Kansas," he said, the shadows from the past darkening his eyes.

"Newton's in Iowa, but I get your point," Rafe conceded. He did his best to keep the memories in the past where they belonged. Most of the time he was successful. Other times the demons refused to be leashed. "Okay, it's not the hell hole we crawled out of, but the town might as well be living in another century. I'll have to go deal with my grandfather's belongings myself."

Hauk reached to pour himself another shot of tequila from the bottle that had been waiting for them in the center of the table.

Like Rafe, he was dressed in an Oxford shirt, although his was blue instead of white, and he was wearing black dress pants instead of jeans.

"I know you think it's a pain, but it's probably for the best."

Rafe glared at his friend. The last thing he wanted was to drive a thousand miles to pack up the belongings of a cantankerous old man who'd never forgiven Rafe's father for walking away from Iowa. "Already trying to get rid of me?"

"Hell no. Of the five of us, you're the..."

"I'm afraid to ask," Rafe muttered as Hauk hesitated.

"The glue," he at last said.

Rafe gave a bark of laughter. He'd been called a lot of things over the years. Most of them unrepeatable. But glue was a new one. "What the hell does that mean?"

Hauk settled back in his seat. "Lucas is the smooth-talker, Max is the heart, Teagan is the brains and I'm the organizer." The older man shrugged. "You're the one who holds us all together. ARES would never have happened without you."

Rafe couldn't argue. After returning to the States, the five of them had been transferred to separate hospitals to treat their numerous injuries. It would have been easy to drift apart. The natural instinct was to avoid anything that could remind them of the horror they'd endured.

But Rafe had quickly discovered that returning to civilian life wasn't a simple matter of buying a home and getting a 9-to-5 job.

He couldn't bear the thought of being trapped in a small cubicle eight hours a day, or returning to an empty condo that would never be a home.

It felt way too much like the prison he'd barely escaped.

Besides, he found himself actually missing the bastards.

Who else could understand his frustrations? His inability to relate to the tedious, everyday problems of civilians? His lingering nightmares?

So giving into his impulse, he'd phoned Lucas, knowing he'd need the man's deep pockets to finance his crazy scheme. Astonishingly, Lucas hadn't even hesitated before saying 'yes.' It'd been the same for Hauk and Max and Teagan.

All of them had been searching for something that would not only use their considerable skills, but would make them feel as if they hadn't been put out to pasture like bulls that were past their prime.

And that was how ARES had been born.

Now he frowned at the mere idea of abandoning his friends when they were on the cusp of realizing their dream.

"Then why are you encouraging me to leave town when we're just getting ready to open for business?"

"Because he was your family."

"Bull. Shit." Rafe growled. "The jackass turned his back on my father when he joined the army. "He never did a damned thing for us."

"And that's why you need to go," Hauk insisted. "You need—"

"You say the word closure and I'll put my fist down your throat," Rafe interrupted, grabbing his glass and tossing back the shot of tequila.

Hauk ignored the threat with his usual arrogance. "Call it what you want, but until you forgive the old man for hurting your father it's going to stay a burr in your ass."

Rafe shrugged. "It matches my other burrs."

Without warning, Hauk leaned forward, his expression somber. "Rafe, it's going to take a couple of weeks before we're up and running. Finish your business and come back when you're ready."

Rafe narrowed his gaze. There was no surprise that Hauk was pressing him to deal with his past. Deep in his heart, Rafe knew his friend was right.

But he could hear the edge in Hauk's voice that made him suspect this was more than just a desire to see Rafe dealing with his resentment toward his grandfather. "There's something you're not telling me."

"Hell, I have a thousand things I don't tell you," Hauk mocked, lifting his glass with a mocking smile. "I am a vast, boundless reservoir of knowledge."

A classic deflection. Rafe laid his palms on the table, leaning forward. "You're also full of shit." His voice was hard with warning. "Now spill."

"Pushy bastard." Hauk's smile disappeared. "Fine. There was another note left on my desk."

Rafe hissed in frustration.

The first note had appeared just days after they'd first arrived in Houston.

It'd been left in Hauk's car with a vague warning that he was being watched.

They'd dismissed it as a prank. Then a month later a second note had been taped to the front door of the office building they'd just rented.

This one had said the clock was ticking.

Once again Hauk had tried to pretend it was nothing, but Teagan had instantly installed a state of the art alarm system, while Lucas had used his charm to make personal friends among the local authorities and encouraged them to keep a close eye on the building.

"What the fuck?" Rafe clenched his teeth as a chill inched down his spine. He had a really, really bad feeling about the notes. "Did you check the security footage?"

"Well gosh, darn," Hauk drawled. "Why didn't I think of that?"

"No need to be a smartass."

Hauk drained his glass of tequila. "But I'm so good at it."

"No shit."

Hauk pushed aside his empty glass and met Rafe's worried gaze.

"Look, everything that can be done is being done. Teagan has tapped into the traffic cameras. Unless our visitor is a ghost he'll eventually be spotted arriving or leaving. Max is working his forensic magic on the note, and Lucas has asked the local cops to contact the neighboring businesses to see if they've noticed anything unusual."

"I don't like this, Hauk."

"It's probably some whackadoodle I've pissed off," the older man assured him. "Not everyone finds me as charming as you do."

Rafe gave a short, humorless laugh. Hauk was intelligent, fiercely loyal, and a natural leader. He could also be cold, arrogant, and inclined to assume he was always right. "Hard to believe."

"I know, right?" Hauk batted his lashes. "I'm a doll."

"You're a pain in the ass, but no one gets to threaten you but me," Rafe said. "These notes feel...off."

Hauk reached to pour himself another shot, his features hardening into an expression that warned he was done with the discussion.

"We've got it covered, Rafe. Go to Kansas."

"Iowa."

"Wherever." Hauk grabbed the cellphone on the table and pressed it into Rafe's hand. "Take care of the house."

Rafe reluctantly rose to his feet. He could argue until he was blue in the face, but Hauk would deal with the threat in his own way.

"Call if you need me."

"Yes, mother."

With a roll of his eyes, Rafe made his way through the crowd that filled the bar, ignoring the inviting glances from the women who deliberately stepped into his path.

He was man enough to fully appreciate what was on offer. But since his return stateside he'd discovered the promise of a fleeting hookup left him cold.

He didn't know what he wanted, but he hadn't found it yet.

He'd just reached the door when he met Teagan entering the bar.

The large, heavily muscled man with dark caramel skin, golden eyes and his hair shaved close to his skull didn't look like a computer wizard. Hell, he looked like he should be riding with the local motorcycle gang. And it wasn't just that his arms were covered with tattoos or that he was wearing fatigues and leather shit-kickers.

It was in the air of violence that surrounded him and his don't-screw-with-me expression.

Of course, he'd been thrown in jail at the age of thirteen for hacking into a bank to make his mother's car loan disappear. So he'd never been the traditional nerd.

"I'm headed out."

"So early?" Teagan glanced toward the crowd that was growing progressively louder. "The party's just getting started."

"I'll take a rain check." Rafe said. "I'm leaving town for a few days."

"Business?"

"Family."

"Fuck," Teagan muttered.

The man rarely discussed his past, but he'd never made a secret of the fact he deeply resented the father who'd beaten his mother nearly to death before abandoning both of them.

"Exactly," Rafe agreed before leaning forward to keep anyone from overhearing his words. "Keep an eye on Hauk. I don't think he's taking the threats seriously enough."

"Got a hunch?" Teagan demanded.

Rafe nodded, as always surprised at how easily his friends accepted his gut instincts. "If someone wanted to hurt him, they wouldn't send a warning," he pointed out. "Especially not when he's surrounded by friends who are experts in tracking down and destroying enemies."

Teagan nodded. "True."

"So either the bastard has a death-wish. Or he's playing a game of cat and mouse."

"What would be the point?"

Rafe didn't have a clue. But people didn't taunt a man as dangerous as Hauk unless they were prepared for the inevitable conclusion.

One of them would die.

Rafe gave a sharp shake of his head. "Let's hope we have culprit in custody when we find out. Otherwise..."

"Nothing's going to happen to him, my man." Teagan grabbed Rafe's shoulder. "Not on my watch."

MICHEL/STRIKER

BY ALEXANDRA IVY AND LAURA WRIGHT

BAYOU HEAT SERIES

CHAPTER 1

Winter was no more than a crisp edge in the breeze that threaded its way through the Wildlands. Michel sucked in a deep breath of the fresh air, savoring the tingle of magic that flowed through his veins.

He loved this secret homeland of the Pantera. It was a place of beauty, power, and untamed dangers that lurked in the thick shadows. Not even the dozen new houses that were being constructed for the victims who'd been rescued from Locke's dungeons of horror could mar the lush wetlands that were filled with a vibrant green.

This morning, however, his attention wasn't on the cypress trees that dotted the thick bayous, or the nearby cubs who playfully wrestled on a patch of grass. Instead he watched the slender female who was perched on a fallen log, monitoring the playful cubs and occasionally making scratches on a clipboard she had balanced on her knees.

She was a striking beauty with her long curly red hair that blazed in the sunlight with a rich gold threaded through the strands. Her eyes were a pale green and her skin was soft and satiny, except for the scars that ran from her mid-cheek down to her throat.

The first time he'd seen her, he'd noticed the burn marks she tried to hide with her hair, but he'd instantly dismissed them. Instead, it was the rest of her satin skin that had captured and held his attention. A perfect cream that made his cat long to lick it until it was rosy with passion.

His intense arousal had set off all sorts of alarms in the back of his mind. Not to mention pissed him off.

This female had worked with Locke, kidnapping and torturing his people, along with innocent humans. And for all he knew, she was still working for the bastard.

It was obscene that his cat would instantly fall in lust with her.

And even more obscene he'd been unable to take another female to his bed since she'd arrived in the Wildlands nearly a month before.

He swallowed a growl as he sensed the approach of his leader.

Like him, Raphael was a Suit, but the two males couldn't be more different. Raphael was tall, with a golden beauty and easy charm that made him the perfect Diplomat. Michel, on the other hand, was three inches shorter with broad shoulders and muscles that bulged beneath the New Orleans Saints sweatshirt and faded jeans he was wearing. His dark hair was skull-shaved and his eyes a dark green rimmed with black. His skin was naturally a deep copper tone, with a tattoo of a crouching puma inked on his chest.

He was also more aggressive than most Suits, which was why his brothers had been shocked when Raphael had made him a spy. But while Michel might not have a golden tongue, or the ability to mix among the humans, he could scale a building, disable the surveillance, and take out a dozen guards without breaking a sweat. Hell, he'd broken into the Oval Office just to prove he could.

"Should I ask why you spend so much time watching Dr. Young?" Raphael demanded, folding his arms over his chest as he studied Michel's tight expression.

"I would think that was obvious," he muttered.

"Yes, I suppose it is," Raphael drawled. "She's lovely."

A strange sensation tightened around Michel's chest, his gaze never wavering from the female. She wasn't lovely.

She was stunning.

It wasn't just the delicate features or the fiery hair. It was the intense intelligence that shimmered in her green eyes and the grim resolution etched on her face.

This female was a survivor.

His cat was dangerously fascinated. Thankfully, his brain was connected to his human side. Which meant he wasn't going to be blinded by a pretty face and perfect tits.

"I don't trust her," he said, his voice hard as he watched her lean forward and lightly run a finger down the nearest cub's back.

Over the past two weeks she'd requested the opportunity to do non-invasive research on the children who had been created in Locke's laboratories. She'd promised that she only wanted to make sure that they were healthy and growing at a steady rate.

"Have you forgotten that she has given us information on our enemy that we would never have discovered without her?" Raphael demanded. "And that her skills have helped us heal our people?"

Michel turned his head to meet Raphael's determinedly bland expression. Were his lips twitching?

Did the annoying shit think Michel's obsession with the female was funny?

"She's shared just enough to earn a place in the Wildlands," Michel snapped. "For all we know she's a very clever spy who's trying to lull us into complacency while she gathers intel to send to our enemies."

"So cynical," Raphael murmured.

"Because it's what I would do," Michel said between clenched teeth.

"True."

Michel made a sound of frustration. He didn't understand why everyone else was so eager to forgive and forget when it came to Dr. Chelsea Young.

She was the enemy.

No matter what his cat might be trying to tell him.

"Besides, she's had Pantera blood. She's admitted that she's developed heightened senses and she's stronger than she was before her injections," he pressed. "And there's that little matter of her claim that she can 'sense' the Pantera. And even humans from a great distance."

Raphael shrugged, not nearly as concerned as he should be. "I know, which is why I have her under constant surveillance."

He nodded toward a large Hunter with short, tousled dark hair and eyes that were a vivid violet flecked with gold.

Far from comforted, Michel growled deep in his throat.

The young male had been lurking around Chelsea for weeks, his handsome features and easy charm easily working their magic on Dr. Young. Usually Michel found Rage's ability to ensnare the opposite sex a source of amusement.

Now there was nothing funny about it.

Not one fucking thing.

"Rage is a talented Hunter, but he doesn't understand the complex games that spies play," Michel pointed out the obvious. "Not too mention he's a perpetual flirt."

Raphael cocked a brow. "Does that bother you?"

Michel refused to be goaded. He'd already revealed more than he wanted. "It leaves him open to manipulation."

"Ah." There was a hesitation before Raphael cleared his throat. "You know, Michel, I assumed you of all people would be sympathetic to Chelsea."

His brows snapped together. "Why would I have sympathy for a woman who used our people as science experiments?"

"Because you know what it's like to be different while you're growing up, and the desperation to fit in."

Michel's breath caught in his throat, his cat crouching inside him as a remembered pain made him flinch. He rarely allowed himself to recall his early childhood when he'd been born with deformed legs. The twisted joints had been beyond the efforts of the Healers, and it hadn't been until human technology had evolved far enough to operate on him that he'd at last been able to walk.

Yes. He understood the dark desperation of being flawed. And the fierce need to do whatever to gain command of your life. And why Chelsea's eyes remained shadowed even when she smiled...

"It's not at all the same," he abruptly denied.

"No?"

His fists clenched. "I didn't sacrifice others for my cure."

Raphael gave a dip of his head. "Fair enough."

Michel turned so he was facing his companion. "When are you going to confess what's going on, Raphael?"

The older male shrugged. "What makes you think something is going on?"

Michel gave a short laugh. "I can sense when you're tap-dancing around because you have a piece of shit duty you're about to dump on me."

"Okay." Raphael grinned. "I need you."

"About damned time," Michel breathed. As much as he loved the Wildlands, he needed to get away and clear his head.

Plus he needed to be doing *something*. Anything.

"You might not be so eager when I explain your mission," Raphael warned.

Michel gave a lift of his shoulders. "Anything is better than sitting on my ass waiting for—" He bit off his words, narrowing his gaze. "Wait. You don't want me to babysit, do you?"

"Christ, you should be so lucky," Raphael muttered. "I have an endless mob of females in front of my house just waiting to catch a glimpse of my precious daughter." He shook his head, not quite capable of disguising his bone-deep pride. "I barely get to hold her unless I steal her from her crib and sneak out of the house."

"Then what do you want?"

Raphael folded his arms over his chest. "Dr. Young gave us six locations where Stanton Locke might potentially be hiding."

Ah. Now they were getting somewhere.

"You want me to check them out?"

"Actually I've had the adolescent Hunters following up the leads." Raphael grimaced. "They need the practice and they've been itching with the need to do something."

Michel was plagued with the same itch.

Feeling as if he'd been leashed was no doubt a part of the reason he'd become so...consumed with thoughts of Dr. Chelsea Young.

"And?" he asked.

"And I just got a call from Jazz in Bossier City," Raphael said, referring to one of the adolescent Hunters who'd shown great promise. "She's heard rumors that a prominent military contractor recently arrived at

Barksdale Air Force Base and set up a secret lab in the abandoned bunkers."

A sick ball of dread lodged in the pit of Michel's gut. Christ. He didn't want to consider the possibility that the human military was somehow involved. It was going to be hard enough to hunt down Locke and stop him without adding in...

No. He gave a sharp shake of his head. He wasn't even going to go there.

Not until they could be sure what was going on.

"What makes her think it has something to do with Locke?" he demanded.

"She thought she caught sight of Locke headed into the base, but lost him in the wetlands that surround the bunkers."

Michel curled his hands into tight fists. Inside, his cat roared with the need to taste blood.

He was going to stop that bastard. One way or another.

"I'll find him," he swore.

Raphael held up a warning hand. "First I want you to discover what his plan is and who's involved."

Michel didn't hesitate. "No problem."

Raphael gave a sharp laugh. "Whatever you lack, Michel, it isn't confidence."

Michel shrugged. He was the best at what he did. False modesty was as ugly as boasting. "You ask, and I deliver."

"True." Raphael paused, a worrisome smile playing around his lips. "But on this occasion you won't have to do it alone."

"A partner?" Michel scowled. What the hell was Raphael thinking? He always worked alone. "That's not really my style."

"It is this time."

Michel stilled, a chill inching down his spine. Something was up. Something he wasn't going to like.

"Who's the lucky Hunter?"

"Not a Hunter."

Michel narrowed his gaze. "A Suit?"

"An expert on Locke."

"Who?" He sucked in a shocked breath as he realized just what his companion was implying. He'd suspected he wasn't going to like what Raphael had to say, but this… "No."

"No?" Raphael's voice was dangerously soft, but Michel was too angry to care.

"You want me to rephrase it?" he snarled. "Hell, no."

ABOUT THE AUTHOR

Alexandra Ivy is a New York Times and USA Today bestselling author of the Guardians of Eternity, as well as the Sentinels, Dragons of Eternity and ARES series. After majoring in theatre she decided she prefers to bring her characters to life on paper rather than stage. She lives in Missouri with her family. Visit her website at alexandraivy.com

Other Books by Alexandra Ivy

GUARDIANS OF ETERNITY

WHEN DARKNESS ENDS
May 26, 2015
ISBN: 978-1420125177
B&N: http://bit.ly/1ExPYc9
AMAZON: http://amzn.to/1EKROZ9
KOBO: http://bit.ly/1FA1rbA
ITUNES: http://apple.co/1NZnQlB
GOOGLE: http://bit.ly/1JvJU6K
BOOKSAMILLION: http://bit.ly/1yc8Dvr

DARKNESS ETERNAL
MARCH 31·2015
ISBN-13: 9781420138979
AMAZON: http://amzn.to/1ACFHOk
B&N: http://bit.ly/1Emy8IQ
KOBO: http://bit.ly/1FXprFu
IBOOKS: http://apple.co/1BSRE31

HUNT THE DARKNESS
May 27, 2014
NOOK: http://bit.ly/1dxG9wz
AMAZON: http://amzn.to/1euRlxQ
KOBO: http://bit.ly/1jhNa8r
IBOOKS: http://apple.co/1EgIyN7

EMBRACE THE DARKNESS:
Amazon: http://amzn.to/1vJIcWW
Barnes and Noble: http://bit.ly/1j8qRqz
ITUNES: http://apple.co/1FJ7spi
KOBO: http://bit.ly/1GJ7d9L

WHEN DARKNESS COMES:
AMAZON: http://amzn.to/1z5UVYu
B&N: http://bit.ly/1kbospL
KOBO: http://bit.ly/1N8JUg3
ITUNES: http://apple.co/1EFSsqZ
GOOGLE: http://bit.ly/1GHo3rI

MASTERS OF SEDUCTION VOLUME ONE:
iBooks: http://bit.ly/MOSibooks
Kindle: http://bit.ly/MOSamzn
Nook: http://bit.ly/MOSnook
Kobo: http://bit.ly/MOSkobo

MASTERS OF SEDUCTION VOLUME TWO:
Kindle: http://amzn.to/1mpqXLI
Nook: http://bit.ly/1bw3FPK
iBooks: http://bit.ly/MOS2ibooks
Kobo: http://bit.ly/MOS2kobo
B&N: http://bit.ly/1Fr61vJ
Paperback: http://amzn.to/1tVOHbC

ARES SERIES

KILL WITHOUT MERCY
DECEMBER 29, 2015
ISBN: 978-1420137552
KINDLE: http://amzn.to/1NZm7Nj
AMAZON PRINT: http://amzn.to/1Cq8K3d
NOOK: http://bit.ly/1JqAGui
B&N PRINT: http://bit.ly/1JRzMVV
ITUNES: http://apple.co/1HZe1T8
KOBO: http://bit.ly/1D2I4YO
BOOKSAMILLION: http://bit.ly/1yc7Ef0
GOOGLE PLAY: http://bit.ly/1z210TI

BAYOU HEAT SERIES
BAYOU HEAT COLLECTION ONE
ISBN: 2940148435235
July 19, 2013
AMAZON: http://amzn.to/1Dho84H
NOOK: http://bit.ly/Xzo2EK
KOBO: http://bit.ly/1O1YxPV
IBOOKS: http://apple.co/1DvHgwZ

BAYOU HEAT COLLECTION TWO
RELEASE DATE: 11/30/2014
ISBN: 2940149957668
B&N: http://bit.ly/12t9WYP
AMAZON: http://amzn.to/1tDWc3J
KOBO: http://bit.ly/1M61VYW
IBOOKS: http://apple.co/1zKbFkZ

ANGEL/HISS
ISBN: 9780986064173
NOOK: http://bit.ly/1vXBSfe
KINDLE: http://amzn.to/1yMWhVf
AMAZON PRINT: http://amzn.to/1F9ZJxL

KOBO: http://bit.ly/1D2M0sw

MICHEL/STRIKER
AMAZON: http://amzn.to/1ydqfqS
AMAZON PRINT: http://amzn.to/1Eptq1s
KOBO: http://bit.ly/1Jzx6MH

BRANDED PACK
KINDLE: http://amzn.to/1IeEwE0
AMAZON PRINT: http://amzn.to/1zQfJ4m
http://bit.ly/1sSqaqa
http://bit.ly/1ztJcT7
http://bit.ly/13i8xnq
http://bit.ly/1O8sqOy

<u>DRAGONS OF ETERNITY</u>
BURNED BY DARKNESS
KINDLE: http://amzn.to/1JUmwA1
AMAZON PRINT: http://amzn.to/1G4cpVy
KOBO: http://bit.ly/1Jfrd6D
IBOOKS: http://apple.co/1zUPABn

<u>SENTINELS:</u>
ON THE HUNT:
ISBN: 9781420125139
B&N Print: http://bit.ly/1FmMLiW
AMAZON Print: http://amzn.to/1b2g3GK
BOOKSAMILLION: http://bit.ly/1KhLEkp

71675553R00123

Made in the USA
Lexington, KY
22 November 2017